THE RHINO'S Rose

A FATE'S FALLS COZY MONSTER ROMANCE

KARLA DOYLE

Contents

THE RHINO'S ROSE

A Fate's Falls Cozy Monster Romance

As the motherless only child of a ruthless mafia don, I was destined to be leveraged, not loved. Until one of the gargoyles on my family's centuries-old mansion came to life...and saved mine.

That was eleven years ago. Since the night he carried me off, I've lived among monsters in Fate's Falls, a mountain town cloaked and protected by ancient magic. Life has been peaceful and safe. I have everything a twenty-four-year-old woman could want... except romance. Sure, I've been on some dates with perfectly nice members of the local monster population, but none of them made my heart race. Not the way Cornelius Reinhorn does.

The hulking rhino man is tall, thick, strong, and dependable. I'm desperate to know if his gray skin is as rough as it looks, and I've spent more nights than I can count fantasizing about that horn on his snout. Cornelius has always been kind to me. Friendly, even, but never more. If only the big monster of my dreams would see me as a womanly flower, ready and willing to be plucked, instead of "sweet little Rose," the shy human who can't squeak out more than single words in his presence...

Prologue

Sicily

Eleven Years in the Past

ROSA

Hovering in the dark hallway outside my father's study, I hold my breath and listen. Normally, I would be asleep in my bedroom at this hour, but my stomach didn't approve of all the desserts I ate earlier, or the extra glass of wine my father let me have since it was "a big birthday."

Every living member of the Falsone family attended the party, plus some of the made men who work for my father, and even a couple dons of other families. My father's toast called it a celebration of my debut into womanhood.

Embarrassingly, he knew the biological accuracy of that statement because he'd been made aware that I got my first period a couple of weeks ago. Keeping anything secret from him is impossible. As one of Sicily's most-feared mafia dons, no one in his employ would dare get on his bad side. The consequences could be deadly.

I've grown up knowing that everything I do—or don't do—is reported to my father. By my nannies, tutors, the household staff, the handful of cousins who are the closest thing I have to friends. Don't ask me why I expected the details of my bodily functions to be any different. I guess because I didn't think my father would care to know that I got my first period. We've never been close. I honestly can't remember the last time he hugged me.

Isabella, my nanny since forever, the closest thing I have to a mother figure, says my father holds himself apart from me to protect me.

Since I literally never leave our heavily guarded compound, I'm safe from physical danger. As for protecting me from the harsh truths of being a mafia family, why do that when I'll need to learn all about the inner workings so I can take over one day? My mother died when I was just two years old, and I'm an only child. If my father had plans to remarry and make babies until he has a son, he would have started long ago.

Now that I'm officially a woman in his eyes, maybe I should tell him I'm ready to step into the role of heir. The worst he can say is no, right? When I heard his voice from down the hall, I thought this might be as good a time as any to make the suggestion. Until I heard the second male voice, Nicolo Nicchi's unmistakable rasp.

"Not until she turns sixteen. That was the deal." The metallic *ting* of a flip lighter opening punctuates my father's evenly spoken words, followed by the familiar inhalation and exhalation sounds of his cigar habit.

"Yes, Angelo, that *was* the deal," Nicolo, one of the other family dons in attendance earlier, answers. "But you wouldn't have invited me to her party and presented her as a woman if you didn't intend to give her to me sooner."

Give me to him?

"She's thirteen years old, Nicolo. She's not even a full month into womanhood."

Oh my god. It's not bad enough that my father knows my brand-new menstrual cycle, he's sharing that information with the head of one of the other families? That's just—

"I assume that means she is untouched?" Nicolo has the audacity to ask.

Again, I hold my breath, this time waiting for the crack of my father's fist on Nicolo's jaw.

It never comes. Only my father's cool, calm voice. "Not so much as a kiss. I ensure she never has opportunity for any intimate contact with others, just as we agreed."

Just as they agreed? What the hell?

"Good, good. I want her pure in every way when I take her."

"When she's *sixteen*, Nicolo. I gave my word, here in this room, and I will keep it—three years from now."

"Surely you aren't attempting to intimidate *me*, the person who handed you Giuseppe Morello's head on a platter, quite literally, so that you could take control of his territory. That offering was personal, Angelo. I crafted it with my own hands."

I cup my hand over my mouth as the contents of my stomach lurch upward. My father promised me to Nicolo in exchange for expanding the Falsone family's territory? I had just turned ten when that happened. I remember Nicolo coming to the house with a present I thought was a birthday gift for me, but he took it into my father's study instead, and I never saw it again. Now I know what was in the box. And I understand the weird comment Nicolo made when he walked past me on his way out of the house.

"I will see you in six years, little girl."

Only now, Nicolo wants to shorten the timeline.

"I am amending the terms of our deal, Falsone, and if you say another word in rebuttal, yours may be the next head I deliver. Many have offered greater prizes than yours, but I declined those proposals out of respect for our agreement. I am here, my betrothed is ready, and I'm not leaving without what is mine. Wake her now, before I lose my patience. I'm sure you would rather my mood is one of tolerance when I take my bride-to-be to her new home."

My father won't let it happen. Promising me to a creepy old man is bad enough. Letting him have me when I just turned thirteen... he wouldn't do such a horrific thing. Not to his daughter. We aren't close, but I'm still his flesh and blood. His only child.

My pulse is pounding so loud in my ears, I barely hear my father's long, resigned sigh. But his words are crystal clear.

"Help yourself to a brandy and a cigar, Nicolo. I'll wake Rosa and get her ready to go."

No. I must have heard him wrong. He wouldn't. *He wouldn't.*

But he did, and his footsteps on the polished marble floor in his study are headed this way.

Quickly backing away from the door, I bump into one of the obscenely large vases my father favors, sending it crashing to the floor in the dark. Lights come on as everyone—my father, Nicolo, and any staff within earshot of this part of the house—all become immediately aware of my lurking presence.

"Rosa!" my father calls out as I turn and run as fast as possible in my shin-length nightgown. When I don't stop, his tone turns to thunder. "Come back here this instant!"

"I'm not going with him!" I scream as I take the first set of stairs toward my third-story bedroom.

Loud male voices drift up the wide, marble staircases, but they're not directed at me. Father and Nicolo speak to each other in heated conversation. Hope flickers inside me when I hear my father command Nicolo to wait, only to have that hope die seconds later when it becomes clear he means "wait in the study" and not "wait until she turns sixteen."

My pulse skyrockets at the sound of heavy footsteps on the stairs below. Sparing a glance back is a mistake that costs me more than the split-second it takes. With my head turned, I don't see Isabella as I round the corner toward my room, the impact taking us both to the ground.

"You have to help me," I screech while untangling my limbs from hers, then rush into my room.

"Rosa, calm down," she says, following me into the room.

"Close the door. Hurry, help me shove the dresser in front of it. We can't let my father in."

"That dresser is made from black ironwood and weighs more than both of us put together, and I'm not at liberty to lock your father out of any room. Take a breath and tell me why you're upset. I heard you yelling. Did you have another night terror?"

It's been years since the last time, and even now, I'd swear to God the creature I used to see outside my window at night was real, not a figment of my subconscious mind. "No," I say, shaking my head forcefully enough to rattle my brain. "My father made a deal with Nicolo Nicchi—a deal *for me*. You have to help me get away from here."

Her patient expression pales, her lips forming a straight line. "I care about you dearly, but you know I can't help you with this."

Of course not. My father would literally kill her on the spot if she helped me escape.

"Then distract him while I sneak out. You can tell him I pushed you and you fell and lost consciousness for a couple of minutes. Or just...make up any story you need to save yourself after I'm gone, but please, *please*, Isabella, help me get away. He *gave* me to Nicolo. As a wife! He's letting Nicolo take me away tonight. Right now."

"It wasn't 'gave,' Rosa. An arrangement was made. Nicolo swore a blood oath to keep you safe and ensure you want for nothing when you become his wife."

"I'm not marrying anyone because my father tells me to. Especially Nicolo. Why would he think I would go along with that? Why do *you*?"

"Because in this matter, there is no choice. Arrangements are an integral part of the business among the families. Your parents were arranged. Their feelings toward each other were irrelevant. They did what was required, as you will now."

Is that why my father didn't care that my mother died when I was a toddler, because they were arranged and he didn't love her? Possibly didn't even like her? Is it why he never saw me as anything other than an asset to be leveraged for power?

But the worst part, the thing that actually hurts my heart right now, is that Isabella knew about the deal. For the past three years, the nanny who basically raised me has known I was living on borrowed time, that when I turned sixteen, I'd be shipped off to marry a man older than my father. She knew and she's okay with it.

"I don't feel well." Clutching my stomach, I sit on the edge of my bed. "Would you get me a glass of water and a seltzer tablet from the bathroom?"

"Of course," she says, gently stroking my hair. "Then I will help you get ready for the next chapter of your life. There are things every woman should know before her first time with a man."

A sex talk in preparation for losing my virginity to a disgusting, fifty-year-old mobster who decapitated a man in exchange for my body. If I didn't need to get the hell out of here immediately, I might actually vomit.

Groaning and rocking dramatically, I watch Isabella cross the large bedroom. The instant she disappears into the adjoining, oversized bathroom, I bolt for the narrow French doors that lead to my balcony. Throwing them open, I lunge onto the small concrete terrace overlooking the courtyard. There's no way down. Not that I can walk away from.

"Rosa Angela Maria Falsone."

I jump at the sound of my full name spoken in anger. A breeze lifts my hair as I turn to face the room, but the shiver that runs its unwelcome fingers up my spine has nothing to do with the night's cool temperature. "I'm not going with him!" I yell, pointing at Nicolo, where he stands at my father's side, openly ogling me.

Disgusting creepy man.

My father isn't much better, bartering me off like a commodity. Like a whore.

"You'll do as you're told, Rosa. By me, and when you leave here, by Nicolo. Now, get in this room and pack a bag. I'll have the staff box up the rest of your things and send them along next week."

"Fuck you! Both of you! And fuck you too, Isabella," I scream when she enters my view.

"Insolent little thing. But not for long. I'll teach her the obedience you clearly have not, Angelo." Nicolo's eyes sparkle as he rubs his palms together, taking a step forward.

My father blocks him with an outstretched arm, but Nicolo brushes it away, like an annoying fly from a dinner plate. And my father lets him. He lets this, this, would-be child molester move closer.

"I'm not going with you," I shriek, edging backward until I bump against the concrete railing.

"No?" Nicolo mocks. "Then where are you going? Does my little bride think she's a bird that can fly away?"

"I will *never* be your bride, and I can't fly, but I can die. And I choose death over a life with you."

Nicolo scoffs, his eyes opening wide when I yank the hem of my nightgown to my hips, then hoist myself over the railing, where I cling to the other side, my toes barely gripping the narrow concrete ledge. "Enough of this foolish, bratty game. Get in here before you scrape yourself. If there are to be any red marks on you, they'll be from my hand when I put you over my knee for this unacceptable show of disrespect."

Inside the room, my father and Isabella watch in silence. Nobody is coming to my rescue. There is truly only one way out of my father's deal.

"You can spank my cold, dead ass," I say, then spit on the balcony and let go of the railing.

Screams and hollered words fill the air, along with a thunderous, inhuman roar. My hair whipping upward around my face isn't enough to block the impossible sight from view.

The creature from my childhood night terrors comes to life in that instant. His gray, stony body breaks free from the side of the house, quadrupling in size right before my eyes. Massive wings wide, he swoops down, catching me before shooting high into the night sky, with me in his thick, humanlike arms. Saving me? Whisking me away for a worse fate than I jumped to escape?

Or maybe I'm lying dead on the flagstone patio, and this is a dream. The last one I'll ever have. If it is, at least it didn't end with Nicolo dragging me away and doing disgusting things to me. No matter what the huge, gray, flying creature does, I'd choose this monster from my imagination over that real-life man. Even so, a scream rips loose when the last dots of light on the solid land below us disappear from view, replaced by endless darkness.

"You are safe now, Rosa. No harm will come to you."

The monster is speaking to me. Addressing me by name.

My shrieking morphs into maniacal laughter. "I really am dead, and you're an angel." My next breath comes out as a sharp gasp. "Will my mother be there, wherever we're going?" Just thinking about seeing her breaks open the dam inside me, the tears flowing as sobs rack my body. "I don't care that I died if I get to see my mother."

The monster's arms pull me closer against his cool, rough skin. "I'm sorry, Rosa, but your mother is not waiting where I'm taking you. She died eleven years ago, and you are still very much alive."

"How do you know when she died?" The night's cool wind dries my tears as quickly as they stream from my eyes, causing tracks of tight skin down my cheeks.

"I was there. I have always been there, since long before you were born."

"By 'there,' you mean on the side of the house? That concrete statue outside my room?"

"The specifics of 'there' have varied, but my place has always been at your family's side, and yes, that was my stone form."

"Riiight. You're *actually* the monster I imagined outside my window when I was little, and now you're magically flying me off to safety somewhere." More hysterical laughter erupts from inside me. "None of this is real. And it's way too vivid to be a dream, so… what? I hit the ground and now I'm in a coma or something, and this is all subconscious brain activity?"

"I am not a figment of your imagination or a character from a dream, and you are not comatose. You are alive and awake, high above the Tyrrhenian Sea, on your way to a place where no one will ever find you or harm you or force you to do anything against your wishes. My name is Garion. I am a gargoyle, and I have always been real. Those times you thought you saw me, you were correct. It pained me to remain in stone, listening while you implored your caregivers to believe you, doing nothing to validate your pleas. I am deeply sorry for my part in the loneliness you endured."

Shifting position in the monster's arms, I look up and find a pair of intense yellow eyes staring at me. "Whether I'm dead, comatose, or dreaming, this is way beyond anything I've ever imagined. I should be screaming my head off, but I'm not scared of you. I'm not even afraid you might let go and drop me into the sea. I've obviously had a psychotic break."

"Neither your mind nor eyes are deceiving you, Rosa. You're not afraid because inside, you know you have nothing to fear from me. I am your family's sworn protector."

"But you're not protecting my father right now. And I assume you're on his payroll, since everyone at the house is. Everyone does his bidding without question." Betrayal stabs at my stomach as Isabella's complicity replays in my mind like a scene from a horror movie that you can't look away from, no matter how much you try.

"I am not *paid* by anyone." For a couple of seconds, Garion's yellow eyes flicker white, speaking the word *paid* as if it's repulsive. "My oath is to the Polizzi family."

"That's my mother's maiden name."

"I have guarded your family, her family, for many generations."

"Did she know about you?" My whispered words

are barely audible over the steady beating of his wings in the night.

But he hears them. "Yes. But not until it was too late, when I was unable to save her."

"But you tried?" I ask as fresh tears spill, blurring my view of my rescuer's stoic expression.

"I did what I could."

The lump in my throat makes answering impossible, so I nod instead, blinking rapidly to clear my vision. I was only two when it happened, but Isabella told me the basics. My mother had a seizure, fell, hit her head, and died on the same balcony where I jumped.

Of course, Garion couldn't save her; he's a gargoyle, not a paramedic. Plus, it happened during the daytime, while he would have been in stone form.

Isabella said my crying brought her running to the nursery—my bedroom—where she found me wailing over my mother's lifeless body.

Though, maybe that's not even true. Now that I know Isabella's loyalty was always to my father, and that my parents' marriage was just a mafia business arrangement, my mother's tragic death could be a lie. For all I know, my father had her killed. Or did it himself.

I don't know what's real anymore, and the only one who might be able to tell me is a monster straight out of a fairy tale. I have truly lost my mind. "All of this is impossible."

"And yet, you know it is not. Since a very young age, you have known there is more in the world than can be seen on the surface. You consciously remember the nights you saw movement outside your window, the nights you witnessed me returning to the stone after stretching my wings. But search deeper in your memories, Rosa. Remember the first time you looked into my eyes. The first time I carried you to safety in these arms."

"What? You mean—no, that's—that didn't happen."

"You were very small. Barely two years old. Perhaps too young to remember," he says, turning his attention to the dark sky ahead.

Barely two years old.

She died eleven years ago.

I did what I could.

It's as if a door unlocks inside me. The memories rush through all at once. Flashes of sunlight casting ribbons on my beautiful mother's smiling face. Melodic singing. Laughter, hers and mine. Joyfulness. Then the sensation of falling. A baby's fearful wail—my wail. Darkness enveloping me, blocking the sunlight. Cool arms holding me, then gently releasing me. Sorrowful yellow eyes meeting mine before disappearing, seemingly to nowhere.

"She was dancing with me on the balcony. You were there."

Garion's yellow gaze meets mine again. "You remember."

"Just bits and pieces, but enough," I whisper around a gulping sob. "I remember her face. Her voice. I don't want to forget again."

"You won't." Cupping my head in one large, claw-tipped hand, he tucks my cheek against his chest. "Rest now, child. We have a long journey ahead. Plenty of time to talk about the world as you will soon know it."

"Thank you for saving me...twice." Fatigue like I've never experienced rushes in, pulling my eyelids closed. Whatever dreams might come, I know the monster will protect me.

One

Eleven Years Later

Fate's Falls

Somewhere in the mountains of British Columbia, Canada

ROSE

"Don't forget to stop back and let me know how Petra likes the flowers," I call to Kamen as he leaves the shop with a bouquet that's not small by any means, yet is nearly engulfed by his hand.

The massive man turns enough to give me a nod,

then he's off, and I am finally, blissfully, alone in the store.

I'm grateful to be busy, obviously. Rose's Garden has been open for just over three years and is growing steadily—no pun intended. Being able to make a profession of my passion for plants is an honor and a thrill. But today I would trade money in the bank for free time to look out the front window.

As soon as the door closes behind the stone man —and I do mean that literally—I hurry to the bay window that takes the remaining width of my narrow shop on Fate's Falls' main street. Fiddling absentmindedly with the displays will look believable enough to anyone who might pass by. Or to the man I'm watching, should he happen to look over here.

Which he hasn't done. Not once all day.

And why would he? First of all, he's working. Very hard, if the bulging muscles are any indication. Secondly, he's not my customer. Not a single purchase, ever. The only time Cornelius has set foot in my shop was at its grand opening, and that appearance didn't count since nearly everyone in town showed up to support me.

The optimistic part of me hopes that Cornelius's lack of patronage at my shop means there's no one in his life he cares about enough to get them flowers. The logical part of me knows that's wishful thinking. Cornelius is big, burly, and radiates virility. He's also well-spoken and personable. The odds of him flying solo all the years I've known him are low.

Yet, I've never seen anyone on his arm or even holding his hand. Nothing resembling a date in the five years he's lived next door to me.

The residents of Fate's Falls are all good folks—it's literally impossible to be here if you're not—but it's still a small town and not much remains a secret inside the magically protected boundary.

As my friend Alexis always says: The gossip is never malicious, but it's often delicious.

If I had a shot with Cornelius, I would totally give everyone something to talk about. I'd be *all over* that big hunk. There'd be no question in anyone's mind that Cornelius and I were a hot-and-heavy couple— something I'm sure my adoptive father wouldn't particularly love.

Not because Garion doesn't want me to date; he does, I'm just not sure he'd approve of me dating our neighbor. Though, he hasn't been enthusiastic about the handful of locals I've dated in the past few years, either. Those suitors were all perfectly fine. But "fine" doesn't make my heart race or my body tingle.

Just thinking about Cornelius does both of those things. He's always had that effect on me, since the first time we met, when I was nineteen years old.

I was out in the backyard of the house Garion and I have lived in since arriving in Fate's Falls, working in my garden, when the sound of him talking to someone who had the deepest bass I'd ever heard broke through my daydreamy state. I assumed the voice must Garion's gargoyle brother Guillaume, whom he hadn't seen in six years and had just heard from the week before. Naturally, I brushed the dirt off my hands and headed around to the front of the house to meet my sort-of uncle.

And came face-to-face with Cornelius instead.

By that point in my life, I'd seen a lot of creatures of varying shapes and sizes. But I'd never seen a rhino man. I couldn't even say hello to him because my jaw was hanging open. From the prominent single horn on his snout to his wider-than-a-door shoulders, barrel of a chest, massive hands, then all the way down his long, thick legs—I just stood there, speechless and checking him out. It wasn't until he apologized for frightening me that I snapped to my senses.

"Oh, I'm not scared, not even a little bit," I'd said, obviously a little too breathily, because Garion cleared his throat in the way only a gargoyle father figure can do.

For a fleeting moment, I would've sworn Cornelius's small, brownish-gray eyes twinkled. Then I blinked, and the sparkle was gone.

Cornelius moved into the house next to us that day, and hasn't given me a hint of twinkle since. He's been friendly toward me in the way neighbors are—or more accurately, the way adult neighbors are toward children. *"How's sweet little Rose doing? Is your dad around?"* His two go-to sentences anytime he has to do more than raise his hand to wave at me.

Two sentences that could be casual, but always strike me as pointed. Like he wants to make sure his stance of seeing me as the innocent daughter of his neighbor is never in question. Even now that I'm twenty-four.

Sighing, I shift position at the bay window so I have the best view of Cornelius lugging massive rocks into the store that's under renovation across the street. He bought the masonry business from its previous owner when he moved to Fate's Falls. Sometimes he does the business-y stuff, other times he's on the jobsite with the crew of two he inherited.

I'm glad today falls into the "other" column. If I can't have the physical contact I've fantasized about, at least I get a good view of his thick, gray deliciousness for a few hours.

Or, make that a few minutes, since another customer is headed directly toward my shop. Ogling Cornelius's mouthwatering physique will have to wait.

"Hi Lexi," I say as the bell over the door chimes her entrance. Despite my frustration at the interruption of my stalking, the smile I give her is genuine.

There are several witches in Fate's Falls, each nice in their own way, but Lexi Goodwin has been my favorite since the first time I met her—even though she wouldn't bend the rules and let me into her store before I turned eighteen. Back then, I was only curious to see all the magically infused dildos on the shelves at Every Witch Way.

After I met Cornelius, I had a more specific reason for wanting to check out Lexi's inventory. To my incredible disappointment, she didn't—and still doesn't—stock a rhino-man dildo. All of her products are created from molds of living creatures who've entered a license agreement, and to this day, she hasn't had the opportunity to mold a rhino man's cock.

Meaning, I still don't know what one looks like, or how big it might be. Based on the size of every other part of Cornelius, I bet his cock is huge. Maybe too huge for a human-sized woman to take. It's possible that's the reason I've never seen him on a date. Fate's Falls is home to a lot of species, but there are no rhino women in town.

"Yoo-hoo, Rose…" A green hand waving in front of my face accompanies the sing-song tone.

"Oh, sorry." I blink my attention away from the flower shop's front window. "I kind of zoned out there. Not enough caffeine this morning, I guess."

Black-as-pitch eyebrows rise over glittering green eyes, and her lips curve into a knowing smile. "We both know you weren't zoned out, you were *zoning in* on the delectable hunk of rhino-liciousness," she says, pointing one purple-lacquered finger toward the window.

Jealousy slithers up my spine, but only for a split-second. Lexi is older than me, beautiful, outgoing, upfront and honest about literally everything, and makes no secret of being pro sexual enjoyment. She wouldn't tease me about eyeballing Cornelius if she were interested in him.

"Have you taken this prime opportunity to get closer to him?" she asks when my response to her insinuation is silence.

Not only silence, there's also a full-face blush happening, based on the heat flaring beneath my cheeks and forehead. The fair complexion that goes with being a redhead doesn't pair well with my tendency toward embarrassing easily.

Lexi's long, ebony hair shimmers as she shakes her head. "You've had it bad for that man since the day he moved to town. Maybe he didn't notice you then, but hello, look at you now. You're a gorgeous young woman. So, why aren't you across the street right now, offering him a cold drink and a hot view of your boobs?" She inclines her head, making a circular motion in the direction of my cleavage. "That dress is *very* flattering."

Additional heat floods my skin. This time, in the area currently under discussion. My boobs haven't felt this hot since that time I tried to get Cornelius's attention by sunbathing in the backyard, wearing the tiniest bikini I could find in the shops downtown.

"Thanks, but even if I knew what to do with this

'opportunity,'" I say with air quotes, "the store has been busy all day and I can't just close up or leave it unattended."

"And now I'm the only one here, meaning it's break time for you. Consider me your happy assistant for as long as needed." Before I can process the meaning behind Lexi's words, she cups my chin and draws it down, waves her fingers in front of my open mouth while incanting something in a language that definitely isn't English. "There. All set."

"W-what did you—"

"Off you go!" Lexi says, cutting me off while moving behind me to not-so-gently push me toward the door.

Did she put a spell on my feet? Because I'm walking out of the flower shop like I'm on a mission, despite the rising panic inside me.

Even though the shop has been steady since opening, the traffic on the street is light and careful, as always. There's no risk of being struck by a vehicle when I step off the curb. Nobody speeds here. Dangerous driving—heck, dangerous anything—doesn't exist in Fate's Falls. The town and all the surrounding area within the Oracle's boundary is secret and safe, protected by old, powerful magic. All I get as I cross the main street is a friendly honk and wave from one of the relatively new residents as she drives past.

Like so many of the human women in Fate's Falls,

she's blissfully happy with a nonhuman male. Ro's orc mate isn't the biggest monster in town, but he's huge compared to her. And from the girl talk I've heard on more than one occasion, the orc is significantly over-sized in his...private area.

His private area. That's the best I can come up, even inside my head?

Attempting to talk to Cornelius is a surefire recipe for embarrassment. I'm going to open my mouth and choke on my words, as I always do, only this time will be worse because I won't have the benefit of casual, neighborly proximity. If I walk over to his jobsite, where I have zero business, it's intentional. There will be no hiding behind a car or bush. No dashing for the door to escape. It'll be personal.

I'll be lucky to squeak out my usual hello. That's if he stops working long enough to acknowledge my presence. He might not; I'm just his neighbor. Actually, no, I'm his neighbor's daughter. This whole "offer him a cold drink and a hot view" idea is destined to blow up in my face.

I should turn around and march directly back to my flower shop. Yet, here I am, stepping inside The Brew and taking my place in the short lineup of customers at the town's most popular coffee house and brew pub. Lexi must have put a spell on me. Meaning, I have no free will in the matter.

And...maybe I'm not entirely mad about it. When I make a fool of myself in front of Cornelius, I'll be able to play the "this wasn't my idea" card and blame it on Lexi bespelling me. Cornelius will give me one of those deep, rumbling chuckles that make my insides go from warm to molten in the time it takes to blink. I don't get to hear his laughter or voice nearly enough.

Plus, I'll get a few seconds of up-close time. I'd prefer a less-clothed view—like the ones I get from my bedroom window while he's in his backyard pool—but he's delicious in his work clothes, too. Every time he carries one of the enormous stones into the store they're renovating, his t-shirt looks as if it's ready to come apart at the seams. A girl can hope.

"Rose!" Dela greets me as if we're two friends meeting for a coffee date, rather than a coffee barista and customer. It'd be fake coming from some people, but not Dela. She's the most genuinely sunshiny person I know. Which is pretty amazing for someone with her life experiences.

Compared to Dela, I got lucky. Garion rescued me from the clutches of my biological father's repulsive business associate before anything truly traumatic happened. Dela wasn't so fortunate. She literally died at the hand of her ex-boyfriend before getting a second chance at life here in Fate's Falls.

"We don't usually see you here in the middle of a workday," she says while I scan the beverage menu board. "What a treat for us and you."

"Lexi offered to watch my store for a few minutes."

"Oh, how nice." As the words leave Dela's lips, the

other barista, Shay, snorts under her breath while using the espresso machine behind Dela.

It's no secret that the two women aren't the best of friends. Shay and Lexi are both witches, but from different covens, and with very different magical skill sets—and personalities.

Ignoring Shay, Dela continues on in her ever-friendly way. "So, what can I get for you?"

"Um…" For the life of me, I can't call up any memory of what Cornelius drinks. All I know is that he makes me very thirsty.

Dela tracks my gaze as I turn my head and look out the window, toward the store down the street where Cornelius is currently standing out front, assessing a pile of rocks before picking one up with ease and carrying it inside. "Cornelius is your neighbor, right?"

"Yes, for five years," I say, blinking my attention back to where it belongs.

"Has he told you anything about the renovation he's working on over there? I've tried getting a peek inside on my way past, but the windows are covered up without even a tiny gap in the paper. There's not much that's secret in Fate's Falls, but I haven't heard a peep about who bought the store, only that it's someone new to town."

And just like that, I have a legitimate reason to go talk to Cornelius. A subject to focus on. Maybe today is the day I stop stammering and squeaking in his presence, and have a full, adult conversation with him.

"I don't cross paths with him very often at the house, but I'll take him a cold drink on my way back to the flower shop, and see if I can get any details."

"That's a great idea! Should I make his usual, or do you want to choose something?" Dela hovers one hand over the takeout cups on the prep counter behind her.

"His usual, please," I say, accepting another of Dela's unintentional gifts to me, since I have no idea what kind of drink to order for him.

"Coming right up." Dela gets to work filling a large cup with several liquids, a handful of some sort of greens that look suspiciously like lawn clippings, and—

"Is that *tree bark?*"

Nodding, Dela's smile shifts from general good-natured happiness to what is unmistakably pride. "When I learned that Cornelius is a vegetarian by nature, I did a little research into his species' preferred greenery intake, then modified one of our drinks to include local plants that are most similar."

"That was so thoughtful." Logically, I know the jealousy creeping up from the pit of my stomach is unfounded. Dela only has eyes for one monster in town, and he's not my rhino man. Still, her knowledge about Cornelius is like a little kick in the aspirations. I've lived next door to him for five years and had a crush on him for every single one of those days, yet I didn't know he's a vegetarian, or that it's innate rather than a choice. It's my own fault for becoming a blushing bumbler anytime he gives me even brief, basic attention.

"And what can I get for you?" she asks, setting the tall beverage on the counter. Whatever the greens she added were, they gave the drink an almost neon glow.

"Um…" For a split-second, I consider asking for a smaller version of Cornelius's drink, just to know more about him. Doing that would be the same as confessing my crush to Dela. Definitely not ready for someone else in town to be aware of my unrequited feelings. Lexi knowing is bad enough.

"Orange-hibiscus refresher with coconut milk?" Dela offers.

"Perfect, thank you." I don't come to The Brew regularly, and haven't been in for several weeks, but when I do, that's my go-to drink. "Do you remember everyone's favorites?"

"I try. Years of conditioning I'll probably never unwire in my brain. But now it's my choice to be a people pleaser, and it makes me happy if I can brighten someone's day with a little extra personal touch." As she's reaching for another takeout cup from the dispenser, her attention shifts to the coffee shop's entrance, and her cheeks turn nearly as red as the revenge demon walking through the door.

Fate's Falls is protected by the Oracle's powerful, ancient magic. Only those who are meant to be here can find it, and no evil can penetrate the boundary. Violence and wrongdoing are literally impossible here.

That doesn't make the towering hell demon any less intimidating. If he notices me staring, he doesn't acknowledge it. His fiery gaze never strays from Dela, and hers is just as locked on to him. She finishes making my drink with what must be barista autopilot. It's pretty impressive, really.

"Keep the change," I say, sliding cash across the counter and stepping out of the way.

Silent, her mouth slightly open, Dela gives me a small nod, her focus remaining entirely on Razbunare, now standing in front of her.

It's nice to know I'm not the only person who becomes speechless when face-to-face with their monstrous crush. Still, that knowledge doesn't settle the butterflies that rush to action as I walk down the street toward Cornelius's jobsite. The urge to veer across the road and go back to my flower shop is strong, yet my feet stay the course toward Cornelius. Whatever witchy woo-woo Lexi did when she wiggled her fingers in front of my mouth, it's still working.

The question now is whether my mouth will work when I reach Cornelius. I'll find out in five, four, three, two...

Two

CORNELIUS

One more look I shouldn't have taken, but couldn't resist, and now I'm making eye contact with Rose. And she's headed right for me. Carrying two drinks, one of which is a familiar green, removing any doubt that I'm her target.

"How's sweet little Rose doing today?" I ask while picking up a rock large enough to block the front of my pants. My cock doesn't care that Rose is off-limits; it always stands up to greet her when she's within reach. The rock will hide the monster straining against the inside of my fly. It'll keep my hands busy too, so I don't give in to temptation and tuck that fluttering lock of long, red hair behind her ear.

She's not mine. Never will be. No matter how much everything in me insists otherwise.

As usual, she gets red in the face and shifts on her feet, her full lips parted in a soft little O that I know can make all kinds of erotic noises.

Rhinos don't have the best eyesight, but our hearing is exceptional, and Rose likes to keep her bedroom window open in the summer months. The sound of her soft moans and sharp gasps of pleasure—

"Watching you work all morning made me hot and thirsty." Her answer breaks through my inappropriate thoughts.

My thoughts aren't unusual. Her manner of speaking *is*. She usually gets tongue-tied around me. Not only has she found her voice today, she's using it with confidence. Based on her suggestive tone, the shimmer in her eyes, and flirty smile on her lips, her comments aren't entirely about general temperature and feeling parched.

I'm aware of Rose's crush, but this is the first time she's been outgoing toward me, and it makes resisting her that much more difficult. All I can do is silently stare and hope she gets flustered and walks away.

Instead, she smiles and holds out a green drink. "I got this for you. Can you take a break?"

The thick fabric of my work pants isn't enough to compress my erection. As soon as I put the rock down, it'll be impossible to miss, and while Rose hasn't said much to me in the past, she has always openly checked me out, head to toe. She'll see the bulge of my hard cock and know she caused it. The part of me that insists on claiming my mate is all for that big reveal. But it's not going to happen.

"That's very thoughtful, thanks. You can set it on the window ledge," I tip my head in the direction of the storefront, "I'll enjoy it when I get a chance."

"Oh." The smile fades from her pretty face. "Okay. Sure."

Once again, brushing her off has hurt her feelings. And that thing inside me that *knows* she's meant to be mine to cherish roars its dissent, making my guts knot to the point of physical pain.

"Cornelius?" Worry furrows her russet brows when my jaw clenches involuntarily at the internal assault. "Are you okay?"

When I fail to tamp down the discomfort enough to lie convincingly, Rose moves closer. The rock separates us, but her breasts brush against the backs of my fingers. That's all it takes for a rough groan to escape my mouth. My grip on the rock is firm enough to make my fingertips ache, but even that sensation isn't enough to distract me from the tease of her soft curves against my skin.

"You don't look well. I think you should take a break now, not later."

"I can't," I say, after clearing my throat. I even manage to give a casual, neutral smile. The kind a neighbor gives the off-limits young woman who lives next door to him. "The client needs this stonework completed. The next contractor is scheduled to begin the underground integration on Monday."

Rose's blue eyes open wide. "Underground integration?"

It's more information than I should've shared, but I had to give a reason, and rejecting her again wasn't an option. Not sure I even could, with the mating pull hitting me hard.

Now I have her full attention for a subject that isn't about our never-to-be-resolved mutual attraction. A safe distraction. Everyone in town will know about the new store and its owner soon anyway, and when will I get another opportunity to spend innocent time with Rose? Possibly never, since I make a conscious effort to keep physical distance between us.

"Connection to a natural underground water supply," I answer, keeping it vague as possible.

"Different from regular plumbing?"

"Vastly. That's probably all I should say. Don't want to ruin the grand opening surprise."

Continuing to stand as close as the rock I'm holding lets her, she blinks her big blue eyes up at me. Eyes that are so innocent, yet swimming with desire that's anything but. "Do you know when that'll be?"

"I don't." I also don't know how much longer I can endure her lush breasts grazing my hands before I turn this rock into rubble. "But I better get back to work." Taking a step back, I tip my head toward the cups she's holding, and call up the general friendly tone I use for clients. "Thanks for the drink. Very considerate." My experience with human women is limited, and none of it has been personal, but I've spent five years obsessing over the young woman in front of me. I know what disappointment looks like on her face. In her posture. And I know I'm often the reason for it, including in this moment.

Defeated frown in place, she turns and moves to the window ledge I indicated earlier. The sill is low, requiring she bend over to set down my cup. The above-the-knee pink dress she's wearing slides up the back of her shapely legs, stopping just shy of her round bottom.

Gods, what I wouldn't do for a gust of wind right now.

The air has been still all day, but my silent prayer is answered with a sudden breeze that catches the edge of Rose's dress and lifts it high enough to give me a view of her full hips and juicy ass, barely covered by a pair of tiny, pale-pink panties.

Fuck me. That vision is getting pinned to the top of my memories, to be replayed on a loop, especially when I'm alone in my bedroom tonight.

The show ends as quickly as it began, her dress dropping naturally into place as she reaches around to reclaim her modesty.

I avert my gaze before she turns to face me, acting as if I've been contemplating the rock pile the entire time. "Heading back to Rose's Garden now?" I ask, looking at her when she moves toward me.

"I guess I am." More disappointment laces her soft voice, and again, I'm the one who put it there.

Can't be helped. As her adoptive father has said many times, his sweet little Rose deserves a full, happy, human life. I'd give her the world, but I can't give her that.

ROSE

By the time I step inside the flower shop, I'm stomping rather than walking, and the heat in my cheeks has as much to do with angry frustration as it does embarrassment. Fortunately, the only person in the store is the woman who sent me on the ridiculous mission.

"Whatever spell you put on me forced me to make a total fool of myself. The worst ever. At least when I clam up around him, I'm not making humiliating comments like I did just now, before he politely dismissed me. At least he didn't laugh in my face. Though I'm sure he was busting a gut internally."

From her position near the window, Lexi tilts her head to one side, then the next, her black eyebrows pulling toward the bridge of her nose. "First of all, I did *not* put a spell on you that forced you to do anything. Goodwin witches may play loose with the old-school rules of magic, but there are lines we never cross, and restricting or influencing free will is one of them. And you've known me long enough to be very aware that I am *all about* consent. So, whatever you said to Cornelius, it was entirely because you wanted to."

"Then what was that swirly woo-woo thing you did in front of my open mouth, if not a spell to loosen my tongue?"

Lexi's eyebrows dart up so fast and high, it's a wonder they don't shoot right off of her face. "That was a breath-freshening spell!" First, she snorts, then full-out laughs, the kind that comes from the belly, which she holds with one arm while rocking with unbridled delight.

"You're kidding, right?"

"I do love a good teasing, but I never twist the truth."

"Ugh, I know," I say, sighing. "Want this? My stomach is so twisted up, I don't think I could keep it down." I hand her the untouched drink, then drop into a chair behind the counter and lean forward, burying my face in my dress. "Hey!" I jolt upright and point at her. "What about that out-of-nowhere wind that whipped my dress up? Did you do that?"

Leaning on the opposite side of the counter and

toying with the drink straw, she shakes her head. "I had nothing to do with it. Could've been someone else's magic, or just nature's perfect timing. Either way, it definitely worked in your favor. Cornelius's tiny eyes nearly popped right out of his head. He couldn't stop staring at your ass!"

"He did not stare at it."

"Oh, he most certainly did, Rose. I was watching the whole time. That big hunk is definitely attracted to you. Now tell me—what delicious things did you say to that horny man?"

"Lexi! You do not know he's...*horny.*" The last word comes out as a squeak.

Once again, Lexi's free-spirited laughter fills the store, then she makes a hand-job type gesture in front of her nose. "Does he not have a big, thick *horn* protruding from the middle of his face?"

"Oh, well, yes." Pretty sure my face couldn't get any hotter. I'm probably as red as the romantic long-stem roses in the cooler behind me.

"But don't doubt that he was the other type of horny for you, too. Did you not notice how he used that rock for groin cover the whole time he was near you?"

"It was not for cover," I say, rolling my eyes. "He was carrying it inside the building and I interrupted him."

Lexi makes a noncommittal sound before wrapping her deep-purple lips around the straw and taking a long sip that ends with puckered lips and a wrinkled nose. "Do you want any of this?" When I shake my head, she waves her hand above the cup, incanting a short string of words that change the liquid to a red so dark it's almost black. And there's a wisp of smoke coming out of the straw, as if it were a little stovepipe. "That's better. Now, tell me what you said that you're embarrassed about."

"Why?"

"So I can tell you why you shouldn't be."

"Good luck with that. He asked me how I'm doing today, the only thing he ever says to me. And usually, I choke, and I'm lucky to squeak out a single word answer. But this time, because I thought you'd bespelled me, I said exactly what came to mind—I told him that watching him work made me hot and thirsty."

"Ooh, that *is* delicious!"

"Not really, since he just stared at me. Then I asked him to take a break and have his drink and he declined. He said he's on a time limit to get the stonework done for the new owner, but I know he was just being polite. I need to get over him because he's not interested in me."

"He *is* always courteous and good-natured, and it's true that Delphine has everyone on a strict timeline over there to get the grotto ready, but I'd bet the profit margins of my bestselling dildo that Cornelius has it bad for you. And let me tell you, that model is a big moneymaker. Emphasis on *big*." She raises her hands and spreads them apart, then farther apart.

There's no point continuing to discuss Cornelius. Lexi is a fun cheerleader, but she's reading him wrong. And, as intrigued as I am to know which monster-molded, magically infused dildo she's referring to with her frighteningly far-apart hands, the other nugget of information interests me more. "Who is Delphine? And what kind of business is a grotto?"

Eyes glimmering with signature Lexi playfulness, she taps one long, purple-lacquered nail against her smiling lips. "I only know her first name, and she wiggled her way out of answering the business question when I asked," she says, picking up the dark drink and sashaying her way toward the door. "But I'm sure her grotto will be swimming with delight!" With a wink and a wave, Lexi exits the flower shop, leaving me alone with my curiosity, embarrassment, frustration, and the view of Cornelius and his bulging muscles as he lugs huge rocks into the store across the street.

Three

CORNELIUS

The main town portion of Fate's Falls is walkable to almost everywhere. Beyond that is a much larger area, including fields, forests, rocky outcroppings, and a small but thundering waterfall, all of which is encompassed by the Oracle's magically protected boundary. Inaccessible and essentially invisible to all outsiders, human and nonhuman alike. Only those who are meant to be here can traverse the boundary. That's how it is with all the Oracle's secret towns around the world.

When I felt the pull to Fate's Falls, I hoped it was a sign that my mate would be waiting for me. Why else would I want to leave my home in Kenya and move to a mountain in British Columbia, Canada? At that point, I'd long since reached the age of maturity, yet felt no pull to bond with any of the females in my town. For a decade, I coupled with females, hoping to feel more than fleeting gratification, only to question whether I would even recognize the mate bond if it happened.

The question was answered when I met Rose. Sweet little Rose, that's how her father figure introduced her to me. Every instinct awakened inside me at the sight and scent of the young human woman. I was nearly twice her age and double her size. We were too different, yet I didn't doubt for a single second that she was my mate. Knowing it and accepting it—not the same thing.

I've successfully fought my instincts for five years. Today, I nearly succumbed. All afternoon, I felt her eyes on me from across the street. Gods, I wanted to give her something to look at. To preen and roar for my mate. Except, what's under my clothing would terrify her, not turn her on.

Maybe that's what I should do—let her see how different rhino men are from humans. She wouldn't want me anymore. It wouldn't change my deep-seated yearning for her, but it would be better if she turned away, moved on. Ignoring and rejecting her gets more difficult each time I do it.

Given the hour, I shouldn't have to rein myself in again today. The timeline excuse I gave Rose earlier wasn't a lie, and it was well past her shop's closing time when I finally got away from the jobsite.

My home, along with the one Rose shares with her gargoyle father, are on the outskirts of town. By the time I pull into the driveway, the sun is making its descent, bathing the western skyline in swaths of soft orange and pink that remind me of Rose's hair, Rose's dress, Rose's panties. Thoughts of her are inescapable. I need a stiff drink and a firm grip on my cock. Maybe more than once.

"Cornelius." Garion's voice carries across the still evening air as I close the door of my truck. The gargoyle appears seemingly out of nowhere, his large wings folding behind his back. "Sorry to catch you on your way in from work. Do you have a minute?"

"Of course." I've done nothing wrong, yet guilt curdles my stomach as if it were full of sour milk.

I'm aware that before bringing Rose to the safety of Fate's Falls, Garion served as sentry, watching over her family for generations. In the eleven years he's lived here, not only has Garion taken on a parental role in Rose's life, he's become part of the Oracle's security maintenance team. Even with magic as old and powerful as the Oracle's protecting us, nonmagical backups are in place, as are pre-emptive sweeps. Garion is aware of everything going on within the Fate's Falls boundary.

Making his timing for wanting a chat anything but coincidental. Frankly, it's surprising he hasn't previously pulled me aside to warn me point-blank to stay away from his daughter.

I would have, if I were him.

My stomach tightens further when Garion glances back at the old stone house he chose to make a home for Rose. With my mediocre eyesight and the twilight hour, it's nearly impossible for me to see beyond the windows. Gargoyles have heightened vision, particularly at night, and I don't have to be a mind reader to know he's checking to see if Rose has eyes or ears on this conversation.

Whatever Garion sees or doesn't see must satisfy him, because his yellow-eyed gaze returns to my face. "I'm needed back in Sicily for a while, shouldn't be more than a couple of weeks, but I have to leave tonight. Rose is twenty-four and very capable of taking care of herself, but I hoped you'd keep an eye on things while I'm gone. Maybe check in on her every day, if that's not too much to ask. I know she's shy around you and that might inhibit her from asking for help, even if she needs it. I hate to inconvenience you; I know you're busy with that remodel downtown."

"No inconvenience. I'm happy to help," I say as I withdraw my wallet from a back pocket. I pluck out a business card and hand it to him. "Give that to Rose and tell her she can call or text anytime, day or night, if she needs anything."

"Will do." He offers his hand to shake, gripping mine firmly when I accept. "Thanks for taking care of my little girl. Leaving her in the hands of someone I trust makes taking this trip less stressful."

The knot inside me that eased a few seconds ago cinches tight. If he knew all the ways I'd like to have my hands on Rose, I'm the last person in town he'd ask to take care of her.

CORNELIUS

It's just shy of ten o'clock when my phone pings on the table beside my bed. Without checking, I know it's Rose. I'm not much of a texter with friends and family, and it's too late to be anyone in the business.

After offering to be available, I can't ignore the text. Nor do I want to. I must have a masochist side. Though, after the way Rose looked when she walked away from the jobsite, I doubt she'd message me if she didn't legitimately need help. Either way, I'm obligated to answer.

I reach over to the nightstand and collect the phone, my pulse picking up at the text preview that says "Hi Cornelius, this is Rose." In the seconds it takes to swipe my big thumb across the screen and open the full message, my cock is ready to make a tent out of the thin sheet covering my naked body.

Rose

Hi Cornelius, this is Rose. I hate to bother you again (especially after making a fool of myself earlier), but I was about to take a bath and there's no hot water. Is that something quick and easy to fix, or should I call the plumber tomorrow?

About to take a bath. About to be naked and slippery, the hot water turning her fair skin pink. Groaning, I throw the sheet off and wrap my fingers around my cock, giving it a firm stroke from balls to tip. I jerked off in the shower earlier, but my body feels like it hasn't shot a load in a year. Before I get another full stroke in, my phone pings again.

Rose

No need to answer, I'm going to call the plumber in the morning. Sorry if I disturbed you. I know you had a long day.

I should send a quick "Okay" and let it go. But it won't hurt to send something friendlier than a single word reply.

I was still awake, and even I if wasn't, I
said you could call me anytime and I
meant it. If you can't get the plumber
over there tomorrow, let me know. I'll
ask him as a favor to take a few
minutes off the renovation and pop
over to your house to take a look.

Rose
Okay, thank you.

It's just a text message, but I swear I can feel her disappointment in those three short words.

You're welcome to use my tub. It's a
big one, and there's plenty of hot
water.

I don't expect her to take me up on the offer, but when the message shows as read but no reply follows, regret settles in the pit of my stomach. First, I'm dismissive, then I'm a creepy old monster. My big fingers fumbling over the tiny alphabet, I'm in the middle of explaining that it wasn't meant suggestively when a new message pops up on her side of the screen.

Rose
Is now good?

Come on over. I'll meet you at the
patio door.

Rose
Be there in a couple of minutes. 

Two emojis. The rose one makes sense—it's her name. But the blushing face one? Does it mean something, or is that just how humans text each other? Do I want it to mean something? Yes, but also no. I'm a fucking mess.

The priority now is getting my cock under control before Rose is at the door. Fat chance of that when my mind is running wild with scenarios, all of which include my naked, willing Rose. A couple of minutes isn't enough time to rub one out, and I'm not convinced that'd keep my cock down, anyway. All I can do is get dressed and hope for the best.

I spring out of bed and into the walk-in closet, grabbing the jeans I put on after my shower. The belt is still through the loops, and the jangle of the buckle gives me what'll either be the best or worst idea I've ever had.

Clothes in one fist, I head for the Jack and Jill bathroom vanity and rifle through the drawer for the roll of first-aid tape.

When the options are to deflate or get pushed down and taped to the inside of a leg, you'd think a hard-on would soften up pretty quickly. Not the case. Multiple loops of tape later, I pull my pants on over the uncomfortable solution, throw on a t-shirt, and make it to the back door just as Rose is raising her hand to knock.

Rose always looks pretty. Tonight, waving her fingers from the other side of the glass, her hair up in a loose bun, and dressed in a tiny pink robe that accents her hourglass curves, she's mouthwateringly sexy.

Sandwiched between my thigh and pant leg, my cock puts that first-aid tape to the test.

I slide the door open and motion her into the house without saying a word. If it's rude, I can't help it. It's a miracle I keep my hungry mating rumble from rattling the windows. Especially when she passes close enough in front of me that the minimal amount of silky fabric she's wearing brushes against my outstretched arm. The urge to grab hold of the material and tug it off her body is like nothing I've experienced. Every urge and thought is focused on one thing, one truth, one goal: *mate.*

"Thank you for the offer," she says, her voice snapping me out of the narrow funnel. "I didn't *need* a bath before bed, but it always helps me relax and..." Standing in front of me, her cheeks brighten to cherry-blossom pink, and she shakes her head, making tendrils of red dance against her shoulders. "Never mind."

"Tell me." It comes out deeper than intended. Not

a demand, exactly, but firm. I can't take care of her if I don't know what she needs.

"I know it's literally impossible for anyone from my old life to find me, or breach the boundary even if they did, but this is the first time I've been alone in the house. All the normal sounds and shadows are different without Garion there. You probably think that's another example of me being *sweet little Rose*."

The tone she uses to mimic the term I use makes it clear she doesn't like it. More important in this moment, though, is that she's not here with seduction in mind. She's here for security and comfort. Those are things I can provide without crossing a line.

"I think it's completely normal to feel uneasy when you're not accustomed to being alone. And if it'll help, I can do a walk-through of the house when you go back after your bath."

"It might help," she says, then pulls her bottom lip between her teeth. "Until I'm lying in the dark, listening to all the noises."

Do it, the voice deep inside urges. *Your mate needs you.*

"I have a guest room. You're welcome to stay here as many nights as you want." Just making the offer unlocks some of the tension inside me.

"Really? You—" She cuts herself off with a head-shake. "I'm sure I'll be fine at home."

Instinct demands I insist, but I push it down.

"Whatever makes you comfortable." I force a generic smile into place, then gesture for her to follow me. "Just have one bathroom here, but it's spacious and someone your size could float like a starfish in the tub."

Her soft laugh becomes a gasp when she enters the bathroom. "It's so big!"

"I need a tub large enough for wallowing during the months when the backyard pool isn't an option."

Wrinkles form at the top of her cute nose as she tilts her head. "Wallowing?"

"Much like our wild rhinoceros relatives, my species doesn't sweat. We rely on hydration and submersion to cool our body temperature. Wallowing is our word for a long, deep soak in moderately cool water."

"That explains why you spend so much time in your pool." Again, her cheeks flood with a delicious pink. "Not that I spy on you."

"Of course not." The urge to wink is strong, but I don't want to embarrass her. Especially now that she's getting comfortable talking to me.

She steps farther into the bathroom, her eyes opening wide when she trails her fingers along the smooth, curved lip of the eight-foot-diameter bathtub, then down the outer side of the freestanding structure. "Is this stone? Did you make this?"

"It is, and I did. The stone is local, each one hand-picked from the mountain. Since I couldn't have a natural pool to wallow in, I decided to bring some of the nature indoors."

"It's stunning." Leaning over the side, she runs her palm along the interior. "So smooth. I'm sure there are seams, but I can't feel any."

My chest puffs out at her praise. "There are many, but you won't find or feel them."

"It's really beautiful."

"I'm happy you like it." Consciously deciding not to pursue my mate hasn't removed the innate desire to please her. That motivation will stay with me the rest of my life, even after she finds someone to love. An inevitable future I'm not going to think about tonight. "It will take some time to fill the tub for someone your size—since you won't displace water the way I do—so let me get it started and then I'll leave you to enjoy your soak."

"You mean, my *wallow*," she says, smiling up at me as I step closer to start the water.

Thoughts of joining her in the tub, sharing a long, sensual wallow, rush through my mind. Inside my pant leg, my cock strains against its confinement. "Yes," is all I manage to choke out. Being near her, and this new rapport, makes me feel lighter than I have in my adult life. But it can't lead to anything more than casual friendship.

After showing her where everything is and telling her to use my home as it were her own, I exit the bathroom and head for the kitchen because the living room is out of the question. Sitting with my cock taped to the inside of my thigh would be uncomfortable, if not impossible. The damn thing is still hard. Still fighting the binding. Releasing it from the wrapping is out of the question while Rose is in the house. She can't know how she affects me. What I feel for her.

The sound of lapping water isn't helping my situation. It means she's now naked in my tub. Soft humming triggers my hearing, and my ears twitch as I automatically hone in on her vocalizations. Listening intently, it's clearly not melodic humming, it's the distinct *mmm* of pleasure, accompanied by shallow breathing and quiet, high-pitched gasps.

Unable to resist, I go into my bedroom, hovering beside the closed secondary door to the bathroom so I can better hear every gasp and moan. But that's not the worst I do. Hell no. I open my pants and shove them down so I can free my cock. Grabbing a t-shirt from the laundry hamper, I stuff it into my mouth, then lean against the wall and take the first firm stroke up my rock-hard shaft.

What I'm doing is beyond inappropriate. It's unforgiveable, even if I don't get caught. I'll have to leave town. Get as far from Fate's Falls as possible. Maybe somewhere in the middle of nowhere, to grow old and die alone, because there's no way the Oracle will want me in any protected area after I violate Rose's privacy this way.

I know I should stop, but every second she takes

her pleasure in the next room makes my hand stroke faster, harder. As if it has a mind of its own and my brain is no longer in control of my actions. And when she gasps and moans, clearly reaching her climax, mine hits too, sending ropes of thick cum shooting across the bedroom floor.

Everything goes silent and still in the room next door. My heart pounding inside my chest and my muffled, heavy breathing are the only sounds in my ears.

"Cornelius...are you...out there?" Rose's quiet, tentative question shatters the illusion that my presence—and actions—went unnoticed.

I toss the t-shirt over the mess I made and quietly make my way out of the bedroom while stuffing my cock into my pants. When I'm safely in the living room, I take purposely heavy steps toward the bathroom's main door. "Everything okay? Thought I heard you say my name."

For a couple of beats, she doesn't answer. Then there's water lapping, enough to indicate she's repositioning in the tub, followed by a deep inhalation of breath she probably thinks I can't hear.

This is where I give her peace of mind. "I must've been mistaken. Sorry to disturb you. Enjoy your wallow."

"Oh, I'm enjoying it very much," she says with a light laugh. "Thank you."

Maybe everything will be okay—as much as that's

possible after what I did. I obviously can't be this close to Rose, since I'm incapable of controlling my desire for her. I'd pack up tonight and head out of town if I hadn't promised Garion that I'd keep an eye on things and be available to help her if needed. I'm committed to staying put until he gets back.

My gross overstep of boundaries can't happen again. I'll make sure her plumbing gets fixed tomorrow, no matter what it costs. This is the only time she'll be inside my house. When she goes home after her bath tonight, things will go back to the way they were. Neighbors who occasionally cross paths in the driveway. A wave here, a hello there. Then, when her father returns, I'll leave town and never come back. Right now, though, I need to put space between us.

I'm on my way to the backyard when a shriek, then a thud and cry of pain, fill the air. In a blink, I shift directions, thundering through the house to the bathroom door. "Are you okay?"

"I—" A pained whimper replaces her voice. "I slipped and fell getting out of the tub."

Hands balled into fists at my sides, I have to take a step back so I don't barge in. "Tell me how I can help. Whatever you need."

"My leg hurts to move it."

Fuck. "What about when you're not moving it?"

"Just throbbing, not sharp," she says, then, "it's puffing up, but it's not bleeding or bent weird."

"Good, that's good. Try to stay still. I'm calling Dr. Schaefer right now."

In my few minutes on the phone with Fate's Falls' primary physician, multiple soft whimpers and pained hisses come from the other side of the bathroom. It's a miracle I make it through the call because my instinct is to crush the phone in my fist and rush to my mate's aid.

Keeping my hands jammed inside my pockets, I stand a safe distance from the bathroom door when I give Rose the update. "Dr. Schaefer will be here in half an hour."

"Half an hour?" The frustration in her voice is unmistakable. As is resignation when she sighs and says, "Okay."

This is my fault. The sides of the tub are too high for someone Rose's size, especially when things are slippery. I should've taken measures to ensure she could get out safely. Instead, I was consumed with thoughts of her naked body and the ways I'm desperate to claim her. "Is there anything I can do for you until the doctor arrives?"

"Um…" Her pause lasts long enough to draw my feet closer to the door and my hands from my pockets.

"Whatever it is, Rose, I'm here to help."

"I don't want to make you uncomfortable."

"Yours is the only comfort that matters," I say, bracing my palms on either side of the door.

"I tried moving toward where the towels are, but it hurt and... I'm kind of cold."

Gods, is she asking me to go in there while she's lying naked on the floor? Lying *injured* on the floor, *that's* the detail I need to focus on.

"I'll get a blanket and bring it in, but I'll close my eyes, Rose. I won't look; I give you my word." My cock is not a fan of my word. My cock needs to accept the hard—very hard—truth that it will never get anywhere near Rose.

"Okay," she says with what I swear is that same disappointment I heard earlier, when I brushed her off at the jobsite.

In under a minute, I'm back at the bathroom door with a soft throw blanket hanging over one forearm. After five years in this house, moving around one room blindly won't be a problem. It's basically what I do every night because my mediocre vision is further diminished in the dark.

"I'm at the door with a blanket. My eyes are closed. Tell me when you're ready for me to come in, then which direction to walk and when to stop, so I don't step on you." Not that I think I could. Pretty sure the mate pull I feel toward Rose would prevent me from causing her any kind of physical harm. But she doesn't know that.

"You can come in. I'm beside the tub."

Stepping into the room, I'm bombarded by her scent. Because there are no layers of clothing preventing it from emanating from her beautiful body. Because she pleasured herself mere minutes ago. The mating urge wails inside me, my cock thickens, battling to rise inside the confines of my pants, and it takes conscious effort to keep my eyes closed.

"Keep coming," she says in her soft voice.

If only she meant that invitation another way.

"I'm about a meter in front of you."

I take one more careful step, then stop. Without visual confirmation, I know I'm close, that she's looking up at me. I feel her attention on me. I don't know if the huge hard-on I'm sporting is evident from her position, but if I had to wager, I'd put money on yes. And there's not a damn thing I can do about it.

"Here," I say, extending the arm with the blanket. The soft material slides over my forearm as she draws it down.

"Okay, I uh, I think I'm covered."

She thinks? Not exactly the guarantee I need with my cock threatening to punch a hole through my pants. But that's my problem, not hers. She's innocent in all this. And I *will* send her home with that innocence intact.

"Cornelius? You can open your eyes."

I blink them open, my full focus falling immediately to Rose. Thank gods she successfully covered the majority of her body. Even like this, in a moment when I absolutely should not be having personal, intimate thoughts about her, just looking at her is like gasoline on the constant fire she incites within me.

"Could you get a towel for under my head?" Her question snaps me out of my self-centered longing.

"Of course." Turning away to retrieve a clean, folded towel from the cabinet doesn't give me enough time to fully pull myself together, but a few seconds are better than none. The pinch of reprieve goes up in smoke when I crouch beside her.

Though she lifts her head without asking, making space for me to slide the towel underneath, she doesn't raise a finger to help. Probably out of fear that I'll see her nakedness if the blanket shifts. Her lack of assistance means my hands brush against her hair, damp from her wallow in the tub, and the warm skin at the back of her neck. Sparks run from my fingertips directly to my cock, and I don't react quickly enough to stifle a deep rumble.

Her gaze locks with mine, her perfect copper eyebrows rising over wide-open blue eyes.

"I apologize."

"For what?" she asks.

For the sound of my endless hunger for you, my mate, the only woman I crave and the one I can't have. Not exactly the answer I can give, now or ever. "Stomach noise. Ate a bit too much at dinnertime and I guess it's still digesting."

"Oh." There it is again, the disappointment. "You don't have to apologize for that. Or for anything."

If she knew I just stroked off to the sound of her masturbating in the tub, she wouldn't be so generous.

Maybe she'd be excited, says the part of me that knows she's attracted to me. *Tell her how you feel. Make her yours. It's what fate wants. It's what Rose wants.*

The front doorbell jerks me backward and to a stand. "Dr. Schaefer must've made it earlier than expected," I say on my way out of the room, not waiting for Rose to respond. Saved by the bell, literally. All I can do now is hope that Rose's injury is minor, so I can send her home before I do something I can't cover up.

Four

ROSE

When Dr. Schaefer opens the bathroom door, Cornelius is right there, waiting, his big arms crossed over his broad chest. Instantly, his eyes meet mine, then his gaze drops to where the doctor is supporting me by the arm, and then lower, to where I'm keeping my right leg off the ground.

"What's the prognosis?" he asks in that smooth, deep voice that gives me butterflies and a sense of ease at the same time.

"I didn't detect any breaks or fractures in my physical or sensory examination, though I'd like to see Rose in my office tomorrow morning to do a technical scan, just to be certain. Unless the results prove otherwise, and I don't expect that to be the case, I'd call it a sprain. Because of the swelling and Rose's pain level, I'm leaving some extra-strength anti-inflammatories, and I'll send a script through to the pharmacy when I get home. I'll arrange for some crutches, too."

"Thank you," Cornelius says, nodding. "I'll pick it up and make sure Rose gets to your office at whatever time you need her there. Is there anything else we need to know or do?"

We?

Before I can sputter out any sort of response, Dr. Schaefer smiles at each of us, then hands me over to Cornelius. The way he slides one arm around my waist and holds me close makes it feel like we really are a "we." But I know he's only acting this way out of guilt, obligation, or likely, a combination of both.

Dr. Schaefer continues regarding us as if seeing us together is a regular occurrence. Of course, she knows it's not. She's been my doctor since I came to Fate's Falls eleven years ago as a frightened, shell-shocked thirteen-year-old. According to my friends who've lived in town their whole lives, Dr. Schaefer has been here longer—as in a lot longer—yet doesn't appear to have aged a day. Being a shape-shifter, maybe she has control of everything about her physical form.

"RICE—rest, ice, compression, elevation," she says, pulling a set of keys from a pocket on the outside of her medical bag, then moving toward the front door. "Absolutely no weight on that foot until the swelling is completely gone."

"Got it," Cornelius says. "Thanks for coming out so late in the evening."

"Always available to help if I'm needed." With one last smile, and what I swear is a knowing nod in my direction, the good doctor sees herself out.

Then Cornelius and I are alone. And we're touching.

Knowing he's holding me so I don't fall down or further injure myself doesn't stop my body from responding to the closest contact we've ever shared. Squeezing my thighs together only makes things worse because the hint of pressure is a reminder of the orgasm I had in his bathtub. Something I shouldn't have done but couldn't resist.

I've always been intensely turned on by everything about Cornelius, and being in his house, naked in his tub, amplified my arousal to a will-not-be-ignored level. So I touched myself. And the riskiness of it, that he might hear, gave me a hair trigger. I don't think I've ever come that fast. Definitely not without a vibrator.

Beside me, Cornelius clears his throat, and immediately, my face floods with heat. Not only have I ruined his evening, I'm standing here, leaning on him, rubbing my thighs against each other. And it's *audible*, the sound of my slickness. Because I'm not wearing panties. I didn't come over with expectations of anything other than a hot bath, but I also chose one of my shortest, slinkiest robes and a little slip of a nightie underneath—and nothing else.

None of which Dr. Schaefer questioned when she helped me get dressed. Since telepathy is among her enhanced senses, it's safe to assume she knows everything I feel for Cornelius. Whether it was professionalism or simply kindness, she didn't comment on my wardrobe choice—or its pointlessness, since her telepathy would also give her knowledge that Cornelius doesn't share my feelings.

"I'm really sorry for everything that happened," I say, attempting to extricate myself from his massive arm.

But he's not having it. In fact, he pulls me closer. Tightens his grip on the dip of my waist. "No apology necessary, and what do you think you're doing?"

"Hopping home."

"Not on my watch."

"Okay, I won't argue if you want to help me hop home," I say, trying not to show too much enjoyment of being cared for.

"That's not happening either."

"Then what—are you going to carry me?" The words are still exiting my mouth as heat rushes to my cheeks. "That was sarcasm. I wasn't suggesting you carry me home. Just to be clear."

"To be equally clear, I had no intention of carrying you home."

Ouch. But after all my antics this evening, I had it coming.

"You're staying here tonight." Staring down at me, the corners of his mouth tick up ever so slightly when my bottom lip falls, leaving me gaping up at him.

All I can do is slow blink and make fish faces.

Now, he gives me an actual smile, along with a deep chuckle that might as well be his finger on my clit. "Give me a list of things you need from next door to get you through the night."

Probably shouldn't put my vibrator at the top of that list, right? At least I didn't sprain my wrist.

"While you're thinking about it, let's get you settled on the couch," he says, then, without warning, scoops me off my foot—singular—and into his arms. "This okay? Don't want you to make that injury any worse."

"It's fine, thank you." Fine? *Fine?* I've only fantasized about him picking me up like this since the first time we met. Only, in the fantasies, he carries me to bed. Still, being snug against his chest and thick arms is heaven. Even if only for the seconds it takes to cross the living room.

Placed gently on his massive couch, I can't help shivering at the absence of his warmth. The motion catches his eye as he straightens in front of me. "I'll get you a blanket."

"I don't need one."

His gaze travels over my minimally covered body,

with brief yet noticeable pauses at my breasts, then again at my upper thighs, where the edge of my nightie sits only about a hand's width from my pussy. "You're shivering," he says, when another shudder ripples through me.

"I'm not cold." My hard nipples attempting to pierce the thin satin fabric of my nightgown might indicate otherwise, but I'm sure Cornelius is aware of the real reason my boobs are giving him the double point.

It doesn't take a telepath to know what's going on in my head.

"The back door key is under a small pot of mini roses on the patio table," I say, changing the subject. "But I'll be fine at home if you can help me limp over there. You really don't have to put me up in your guest room tonight."

"I wasn't planning on it. You'll sleep in my bed."

Again, my mouth falls open. My cheeks feel as if they're literally on fire, and the heat from the blush spreads down my neck and across my chest before I can snap my bottom lip closed.

"It's closer to the bathroom," he says, gripping the back of his neck with one big hand, an action that makes his massive biceps pop up deliciously.

"Of course. That's so thoughtful." I smile, nodding as if I understood the reason without being told. But it's fake. The smile. The casual tone. I should accept that he's never going to invite me to his bed for intimate reasons, but the wishing and hoping refuse to die. Even after five years of his polite rejections.

"What do you want me to get from your place?"

"Sorry. You're probably exhausted from working hard in the heat all day, and my bath fiasco is messing up your life." I attempt to sit up straighter to present myself in a more attentive way, and end up *presenting myself* instead. As in, the loosely tied robe falls aside and the slippery nightie slides up my legs. I don't have to look down at my lap to know that the peak of my pussy is playing peekaboo.

But I do look down. And so does Cornelius.

I scramble to tug the nightie into place, accidentally putting weight on my sprained ankle in the process, which results in shrieking and jerking in a way that fully exposes my naked lower parts rather than covering them.

Cornelius tosses a crocheted blanket over me as if he's trying to smother a fire. Then he basically bolts from the room and the house, the back door closing sharply behind him.

I should be mortified. Humiliated. And part of me is, but the other part, the ever-hopeful part... she's victoriously parading around inside me. Because before Cornelius played gentleman hero, he did three things.

He stared directly at my pussy.

He made the sexiest, hungriest, rumbling sound I've ever heard.

And he grabbed his cock through his pants.

Cornelius might not *want* to want me, but his body disagrees. Tonight, I'm going to make sure he knows I want him, too.

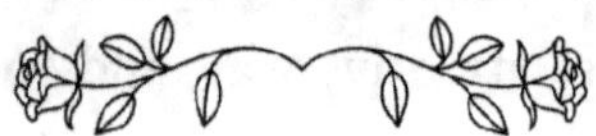

CORNELIUS

Sleep is never going to happen.

I only have a guest bed because the previous owner left it behind. Any time I thought about getting rid of it, something niggled at me to keep it. Ridiculous, since it's a single bed made for a human or some other smaller-framed creature.

Tonight, I learned why I felt compelled to keep the bed—so I could offer it to Rose. And now Rose is sleeping in *my* bed, infusing my sheets and pillows with her essence.

For what has to be the hundredth time since I lay down on the guest bed, I roll onto my right side. Then onto the left. Then my back. Some part of me overhangs the mattress no matter what position I try.

Then there's my damn cock, which has refused to go down since I got an eyeful of Rose's bare pussy. Gods, the sight of her. Pink and glistening. And her scent. I had to get away before I dropped to my knees and devoured her right there on my couch.

She would have let me, I know she would. She would've come on my tongue, then I would've buried myself to the balls inside her. We'd be truly mated. I'd be fucking her and making her come right now, instead of fighting a losing battle for comfort in a bed that would barely fit our child.

The child I'd plant in her belly when I unload deep inside her.

"Fuck." There's no way I'm avoiding the inevitable. I shove my boxers down and take my cock in hand, gripping it hard as I begin to stroke. Wound as tight as I am, it won't take long. Precum bubbles out of me, lubing my hand and making the sound of slapping skin fill the room. I pump my fist fast and hard, pulling the pillow over my face to mute the grunts I can't suppress.

Images of Rose whip through my mind like an obsessed carousel. Her beautiful, fair face, shining red hair, soft curves, and that pink pussy I want to watch stretch around my cock as I slide inside her.

I groan as I erupt like a volcano, spurts of cum landing on my chest and rolling down my still-pumping hand. The last ripple isn't even finished before my cock is on the rise. Jerking off is never going to satisfy the mating urge. As long as Rose is within reach, my cock will be ready for her.

I swipe the cum off my chest and wipe my hand on

my boxers before snapping them into place over my straining, messy cock. As quietly as the creaking bed allows, I rise and move toward the door, grabbing a towel on the way out.

A quick pause at the master bedroom door reveals nothing but the sound of restful breathing on the other side. Good. Bad enough that I literally can't get control of myself, but I sure as hell don't want her aware of my obsessed state.

The snick of the patio door's lock is sharp against the late-night silence. The glide across the track isn't loud by any stretch, but noise I'd rather not be making just the same. After stepping outside, I leave the door open behind me. A sleeping Rose won't hear me out here, but I need to be able to hear her, should she call for help.

At the pool's edge, I glance back at the darkened house, listening for any hint of alertness or movement inside. All quiet, thank gods. I strip out of the boxers and toss them under a chair, then descend the steps, careful not to make even the smallest splash as I maneuver to the wallowing area I built into the shallow end.

I lower myself so my shoulders and neck rest against the divot molded into the pool's edge. The wallow won't alleviate my endless yearning for Rose, but the moderately cool water soothes the physical heat that's been building since she arrived at my door.

With my eyesight, looking out toward the forest

that both my property and Garion's back up to is like staring into an abyss, so I close my eyes and let my legs rise from the bottom of the pool. With my workdays, I'm rarely awake at this hour. Nature's nighttime sounds fill my ears with their relaxing melody. I inhale deeply, pulling scents of earth, trees, grass, blooming flowers, and nocturnal wildlife into my nostrils. I don't want to replace Rose's scent there, but it's best if I do, even for a short time.

I adjust my position to get better buoyancy, exhaling to release some of the tension that's been coiled tight for the past few hours. The low sound of my grunt quickly dissipates in the summer night air. *Past few hours?* Not even remotely accurate. I haven't been anything other than tense for the past five years. When a rhino finds their mate, they're meant to act. Claim. Pleasure. Cherish. Breed. Denying my natural mating urges has been a daily battle.

After everything that happened tonight, it's brutally clear that I've lost. Since I can't follow through on my instincts, I can't be around Rose. As soon as Garion is back, I'll leave town.

Until then, my hand is going to get one hell of a workout.

As if summoned, my cock breaks the surface of the water, its ringed crown like a magnet for my fist. I'm two long strokes in when her scent replaces all the rest. Sweeter than any bloom, it's like a siren call. But I don't turn to look at her.

She'd say my name or clear her throat if she wanted my attention. Instead, she's hanging back, out of my sightline, not making a peep. Watching me, and from the arousal wafting from her, she's enjoying the view.

Gods, I want to give her a show. Let my mate see the full length and girth of my cock, its wide ridges nature designed to pleasure my mate, how it erupts when I stroke it while saying her name. Except I'm not sure I could hold myself back afterward. Not with her smelling so fucking *ready*.

Forcing my hand from my cock, I lower my feet to the bottom of the pool, leaving only my head and shoulders above the water's surface. "Do you need help?"

She answers with one of her gurgled gasps, and I can't help smiling, especially since she can't see it.

"I...I just...I..."

I shouldn't enjoy that she's flustered and embarrassed and turned on. But I do. I really fucking do. "Is there something I can do for you, Rose?"

For a moment, there's just silence. Then, "Yes, actually."

I push off from the wall and turn toward the house. "Give me a minute to dry off and I'll be right there."

"No, stay there," she says, hopping toward me using the impromptu walking stick I made from a broom handle.

The need to protect her surges inside me. If I weren't naked, I'd already be out of the pool. "Do you want to come in the pool—do you think it'll make your ankle feel better?"

"Yes to the first question. But not in the way you mean it."

There's no mistaking that innuendo, and my cock is all for it. Thank gods the pool lighting is subtle enough to make her view of my underwater body parts indistinct.

My night vision is shit, but the shimmer in her eyes when she looks down at me from poolside is clear as day. The broom handle clatters on the stone patio. Then, propped against the pool stairs' railing, she pulls the tie at her waist and lets the skimpy satin robe fall open, revealing nothing but skin underneath.

I barely stifle a groan as she wiggles the robe off of her body. "I think the medication Dr. Schaefer gave you is affecting your judgement."

"Some extra-strength ibuprofen has nothing to do with this."

"What exactly do you think *this* is?" The words croak out of my dry mouth.

"Two consenting adults giving in to their mutual attraction," she says, carefully lowering herself to sit on the edge of the pool with her feet in the water. Naked. Fully, gloriously, naked.

If I reached out my left arm, I could slide it up the

inside of her leg, all the way up. "We're not giving in to anything. I can't."

"I saw you, Cornelius. I saw your..." A soft little sound slips from her parted lips before she pulls the bottom one between her teeth. Totally naked in front of me, yet she can't say the word cock, or any of its equivalents. Clearing her throat, she gives me a smile. "It looked pretty capable to me."

Show her exactly how capable it is. I shake away the voice. The urges and instincts. "It's not that I physically can't. I won't."

Even in the dim lighting, the sting of rejection is written all over her face. "Oh gods. I-I'm so sorry. After earlier, I thought—I honestly thought you—" Shaking her head makes her hair fall around her face like a curtain as she bows her head while hugging herself.

This is it, the moment that ends it all. The rejection and embarrassment that sends her off for the last time. She'll stop looking at me. Stop wanting me. She'll go on to find an appropriate match. Someone who will give her the full, human life she deserves, like her father has often said.

"You thought right, Rose." I shouldn't do this, but when she looks up and meets my eyes, I don't care about right and wrong, only wiping away the hurt I caused. "I won't give in to it, but I am attracted to you."

"Are you just saying that now so I don't feel totally humiliated for trying to seduce you?"

Stepping back from the edge of the pool, I spread my arms wide and assume a floating position on my back, allowing my cock to break the water's surface. Not the full length of it, but enough for her to see it's hard as stone and standing tall like a sturdy tree. "I'm not in this state because I feel bad for you, Rose."

Her wide-open eyes locked on my cock, she gasps, her full lips remaining parted as I lower my feet, removing the monster from view. Then her mouth snaps shut as she meets my gaze, her eyebrows pulling together at the bridge of her nose. "You could still be trying to make me feel better. Maybe rhino men are hard all the time."

This rhino feels like he's hard all the time, that's for damn sure. And it's always because of her. "No, that's not the case. We get hard when aroused, the same as most creatures."

"And you're aroused because of—"

"You," I say, cutting her off. "You're the reason. Every time."

Leaning forward, she blinks her beautiful eyes at me. "Since when?"

Shame floods me like a tidal wave. "My answer may change your feelings or what you want, but you, more than anyone, deserve complete honesty."

"Because I took a leap and literally bared it all?" she says, a self-deprecating smile curving her lips.

"That's one reason." Before she can ask what other reasons exist, I clear my throat and lay bare the truthful answer to her previous question. "I've been drawn to you since the day we met. It hit me hard, and so did the shame. I didn't want to feel that way about you. You were too young for me. You still are. You deserve better than a nonhuman twice your age."

"All this time? You've wanted me the way I've wanted you?"

"I've been fighting the pull toward you every minute of every day for five years," is the wording I choose. Telling her she's my mate, that I've known it since I first laid eyes on her...that's a whole other level of honesty. "Tonight proved I'm losing the fight."

"I'm glad you lost," she says, shimmying along the pool's edge until she's at the curved area made for my shoulders, which puts her directly in front of me. "Though your math is lacking. You're not twice my age. I'm twenty-four and you're thirty-five, and there's absolutely nothing wrong with that. Plus, I was an adult when we met. Not just in the legal sense. The life I came from, the one I escaped, it made me a lot more mature than most nineteen-year-olds, even though you couldn't have known that when we met. Regardless, I was a woman. There's no reason to feel weird about seeing me as one."

It doesn't sound so bad when she says it. Or maybe that's me rationalizing so I can have what I want.

"As for the nonhuman part," she continues, "Does it bother you that we're different? Because I don't care that we're not the same species. You being different just makes me want to learn about you. Like earlier today, when I found out you're a vegetarian by nature of your species. And tonight, when I discovered that your...*equipment*," that last word comes out on a choked breath, "isn't the same shape as a human man's. Which I only know from pictures and the toys Lexi sells in her store. I...I've never seen a real human one. Or any other species."

Gods above, is she saying what I think she's saying?

"I've been on some dates," she says, as if reading my mind. "But I never felt anything, even from the goodnight kiss. When I'm near you, or even thinking of you, though...I feel things. A lot of things."

"I feel a lot of things too." More than just desire. A hell of a lot more. Maybe if I told her about the mating pull, how I know with every fiber of my being that she's the only one for me, it'd spook her. But I can't bring myself to do it, just like I couldn't let her believe I'd rejected her again. For all my five years of good intentions, I'm still selfish. Getting more so with each passing minute.

I move toward her, my big body slicing the still water until I'm standing before her parted legs. Close enough to touch her, but I keep my hands at my sides. "I'm sorry that my attempt to keep you at arm's length made things uncomfortable."

"One thing I've come to realize is that things happen when it's time for them to happen. All those times I tried to talk to you but got tongue-tied means I wasn't ready to talk to you. The times I did things to get you to look at me the way you're looking at me now, but you turned away, you weren't ready to see me this way. And now we're both ready, I hope." Whether consciously or otherwise, her legs part, wide enough to give me an unobstructed view of her pussy.

Somehow, my mouth goes dry and waters at the same time. "Are you sure this is what you want?"

The way she nods, you'd think I asked if she wants to win the lottery. If she says yes, it's me who's going to win the prize, even though I have no business claiming it.

"Rhinos don't have the best eyesight, especially in the dark, so I'm going to need you to say it. Do you want my face between your legs, making you come with my tongue inside you?"

She squeaks, her hands flying up to cover her face. A muffled "yes" comes through.

Unable to resist any longer, I move closer, wedging my big body between her knees and gently peeling her fingers from her face, then holding her small, soft hands inside mine. "After showing me your beautiful body and sharing your heart, you're embarrassed by a question about consent and receiving pleasure?"

"Because now that it's finally, *finally*, really happening with you, I don't know how to act."

"Don't act. Don't think or guess or worry. There's

no right way of being intimate. Just do whatever comes naturally."

"You'll tell me if I do something wrong?"

"I won't need to," I say, guiding her hands behind my head. "Nothing you could do would be wrong."

"At the risk of scaring you off again, you're putting a lot of faith in a completely inexperienced virgin."

A chuckle rumbles in my chest. "Unless you tell me to step back, I'm not going anywhere. Except down, between your legs." This close to her, I can see her pulse point hammering in her neck, and though her scent is still flush with arousal, it also carries notes of nervousness. "You can always change your mind. At any time, any point, just say no, and I'll stop."

"Okay." Her voice is as soft as her touch against the back of my neck. "Can I say start instead?"

FIVE

ROSE

In the years I've lived next door to him, I've heard Cornelius make a variety of rumbles and grunts during various moods and activities, but the sound that rolls out of him now is unlike any other. It's powerful. Hungry.

"I've waited my whole life for this."

"Hey, that's my line," I say with a giggle. "You've only been waiting five years." My teasing tone becomes a breathy gasp when his big, rough hands mold to my waist.

He doesn't answer, just angles his head and leans in close.

Tingles race through me when he presses his mouth to mine. He doesn't have lips the same as humans, but the flesh around his mouth is velvety soft, and the differences don't matter one tiny bit. Firm yet gentle, he sets a rhythm that feels like relief and passion and a promise, all at the same time. It's not my first kiss, but it might as well be. Nothing before even came close.

He slides one hand up my back and into my hair, where he cups my head, his big fingers sensually massaging as he angles me for a deeper kiss. The curve of the single horn on his snout slides through my hair, then the tip of his tongue teases between my lips, waking up nerve endings all over my body, but mostly the ones between my legs.

His hand at my waist glides downward, over the curve of my hip, then onto my leg. He squeezes possessively, then his big palm slides down the inner slope of my thigh, and his fingertips brush softly across my pussy.

"Still okay?" he says against my lips when my gasp breaks our kiss.

"Yes, definitely yes, it's just different from..."

One thick finger splits the seam of my pussy, and he draws it upward, to my clit, which he circles until my hips tip forward, desperate for more. "Different from what, Rose?" When I don't answer, he adds a second finger, upping the pressure and speed, pushing me closer to the edge of bliss by the second. "Tell me."

"Different from when I touch myself," I whisper, digging my fingertips into his meaty shoulders and rocking against his fingers.

Another deep rumble vibrates from him as he rubs me harder, faster, as if he's gotten me off a thousand times before. In a way, he has. "I heard you earlier, in the bath. Your beautiful, sexy sounds made me so fucking hard, I couldn't hold back. I never can when I think of you."

The mental image of Cornelius stroking himself off to thoughts of me snaps the bowstring inside me. Lost to sensation, I press my forehead against his chest, my choppy breaths and gurgled moans swallowed up by his big, solid body.

"Lean back," he says, gentling his touch when my hips slow their jerking. "Hands on the patio."

My pulse skyrockets as he lowers himself in the water until his head is just below the level of my pussy. I do as instructed, bracing myself on the cool stone. Then he tilts his head back and his mouth is *there*, his breath tickling my oversensitive flesh.

Gripping my thighs, he spreads me open, as wide as the curved cutout of the pool allows, then presses his face against me and inhales. Deeply. "You smell so fucking delicious, my mouth is watering."

My eyes roll back in my head when his tongue licks up my seam. Gods. It's like a switch got flipped inside me and everything is turned all the way on.

"Good?" he asks after I groan at his next long swipe that ends at my clit.

"Literally the best thing I've ever felt."

His chuckle vibrates against me. "The bar for 'best' is going to be a lot higher before I'm done."

Before I can respond with words, he licks me again, depriving me of the ability to speak. A breathy moan leaves my parted lips as his tongue teases at my entrance, shallow dips in and out, then travels to my clit, where he presses and circles and flicks until I can barely breathe from the assault of sensations tugging tight.

There are toys that mimic this, and the ones Lexi sells are not only anatomically accurate but also magically imbued to guarantee satisfaction, but I never bought one. Maybe because none of them were a rhino model. But mostly because I've only ever wanted to know what Cornelius's tongue would feel like. And gods, it was so worth the wait.

Just when I think it couldn't possibly feel better, he raises the bar like he said he would. His wide shoulders emerge from the water and he lifts his head, spans my lower abdomen with one of his big hands, and with two fingers, parts my labia to expose my clit. "I'm going to make you come on my tongue now."

Spread open like this, sweet is the last thing I feel. I also don't feel self-conscious. The way he's looking at me, touching me, feels natural, as if we've been together always.

Holding my breath, I watch him flick and roll my clit with the tip of his pale-pink tongue. Wide and thick, it should be too big to hit such a small target, but it's not. It's perfect. Every second pushes me higher, closer. So, so close. My eyelids flutter closed, and instinctively, I reach for his head, wanting him closer. Needing it harder.

The top of his head is smooth under my palm, but I don't get a chance to explore. He reaches up and catches my hand, guides it to his horn, curling my fingers around the thick appendage as he presses its outer curve against my clit. I've always wondered what his horn felt like, and now I know. It feels like heaven. Smooth, hard, erotic heaven.

"I—oh—gods..." Gripping it with both hands, I pull his horn tight against my clit, grinding against it as he rolls it back and forth. "I'm going to come," I pant, moaning as the first wave explodes.

Then that thick, long tongue pushes inside me. Deep inside. Deeper than any toy I've ever used. Soft and hard at the same time. Wriggling, stroking, making sexy, obscenely slurpy sounds.

"Oh...gods, *ohhh!*" I cry out as his tongue touches a spot I've never found, sparking a whole other kind of orgasm. Inside. Outside. Coming and coming. So good, so good, but almost too much. A string of garbled, breathy sounds that echo in the night air rush out of me, then Cornelius's arms are behind me, catching me as I let go.

CORNELIUS

Pride at giving my mate such intense pleasure is short-lived. Thank gods, I sensed her lightheadedness and got my arms around her before she blacked out. "Rose." I rise to a stand while holding her tight against my chest.

"You weren't kidding about raising the bar."

Her soft voice quiets the panic in my chest, enough that I'm able to chuckle at her humor.

"Maybe a bit too high," I say, scooping her into my arms so I can carry her to the house.

"I do feel a little high, to be honest." More humor. A good sign. "Not that I actually know what it feels like to be high. Another thing I've never done."

"There's a dispensary in town. The troll who owns it is very well-versed in all the botanicals, cannabis and otherwise. I'm sure he'd be happy to help you choose the right product if that's another experience on your bucket list." When I say it like that, I can't help wondering if that's all her attraction to me is—a box to be ticked. An itch to be scratched.

Just because her crush on me prevented her from getting involved with anyone else in the past doesn't mean she won't move on in the future. In all the personal things she shared, she never once mentioned love or commitment. And why would she? She's twenty-four. Beautiful, sexy, friendly, funny. She's just beginning to dip her toes into the pool of sexual experiences. Our relationship, if that's what this is, isn't the beginning of forever. It's a stage in her life.

"I think I'll stick with the high you provide," she says, smiling up at me as I pause inside the house to close the patio door. "I've heard stories—a couple of my friends aren't shy about their sex lives—but I thought they were exaggerating." Her arousal perfumes the air, and one of her hands leaves the back of my neck to caress my horn, her fingertips trailing over it while she bites her bottom lip. "Everything you did was amazing. I didn't think *anything* could feel so good."

The pride returns in a rush, puffing my chest out and making my cock stand tall enough to tap against her bare bottom.

Her eyes go wide and she cranes her neck to look down, gasping at the sight of my cock. "It's so—it's—it's huge. It didn't look that huge when you were in the pool."

"Some of it was underwater."

"I…" Her gulp is audible. "Have you ever had sex with a human woman?"

"Never," I say as I cross the threshold of my bedroom. "I never wanted to."

Her wide-eyed gaze darts to the bed. "Do you know any rhino and human couples from before?"

"There were none in my hometown. Very few humans live there." I carefully place her on the bed, then settle alongside her, close enough to feel her warmth and breathe in her scent, while leaving enough gap to make it clear I have no expectations.

"Then...how are you sure we can...you know, fit?" she whispers, taking my hand and drawing my arm across her waist.

"Will you think less of me if I tell you I did research?"

"Only if you think less of me for admitting I've repeatedly asked Lexi if she could get a rhino dildo in stock at her store, so that I could see one." Even in the sliver of moonlight from the window, her face glows with a rosy blush.

"I'm glad she never got one," I say, leaning over to give her a quick kiss. "It might've scared you off, then you wouldn't have had a plumbing emergency that required you to come over for a bath tonight."

She sucks in a breath, her mouth stuck in a wide O as she stares at me. "You think I lied about the hot water just so I could come over and try to seduce you? I mean, it's a pretty great idea, but not one I thought of. There's no hot water at my house. Let's go over there right now so you can see for yourself."

Amusement rumbles in my chest, hard enough to shake the bed. "We're not going anywhere," I say, pulling her against me when she moves as if to get off the bed. "I was just teasing, my sweet Rose."

She *hmphs,* her copper eyebrows scrunching together. "You left out *little.*"

"Because you don't like it," I trail my fingers

down the side of her face and along her bottom lip, "and I don't like hurting you. I'm sorry I did so many times."

"Oh," she says softly. "Thank you."

When a long yawn stretches her pretty lips wide, I pull the covers over her and stroke her silky hair until she sighs. "Get some sleep. Call my name if you need anything during the night."

Her eyes pop open, her warm, delicate fingers tightening around my forearm. "Why are you leaving? Is it because I got a little freaked out by the size of your…"

Gods, I want her to say cock. But if she did, it'd make it that much harder to go. "Nothing to do with that."

"Then why?"

"This is your bed tonight. You're here as my houseguest."

"Aren't we more than guest and host now? Or was it just a onetime, spontaneous moment out by the pool?"

Tell her, the voice inside me demands. *Tell her she's your mate, your everything.*

"We're more now," I say instead, pushing the mating pull down, as I've done for the past five years.

"Then…stay? If you want to. No pressure. And I don't expect you to cuddle—"

I cut her off with a brief kiss. "I would love to stay here with you."

"I'd love that too," she says, wrapping her arms behind my neck and smiling up at me.

Love. The word exchanged so easily between us holds depth for me. Truth. Love is commitment, connection, fibers in a bond, all of which I have for Rose. But not everyone reveres the word love in this way. For many, it has lost its value.

Logic can wait for another day, one when Rose doesn't want to share my bed.

"Do you like cuddling?"

The quiet laugh she makes is clearly not rooted in humor. "I honestly don't know. My mother died when I was two; I have no memories of her. My biological father is the cold and ruthless head of a mafia family who saw me as currency, nothing more. He bartered me to another mafia don when I was a young child, and had no problem handing me over to be *claimed* as a bride on my thirteenth birthday. Garion is wonderful and I'm eternally grateful he rescued me that night, but I was thirteen when he stepped in as a father. Hugs are the extent of our physical affection. And I already told you about my minimal romantic experience." Her arms slide from me to the bed, and she shrugs while blinking up at me.

"Would you like to try cuddling, see if you like it?" This close to her, I see her jaw and throat move as she swallows hard before giving me a nod. "I'm new to this, too. How do you want to start? What would be most comfortable for you and your sore ankle?"

The giggle she makes now is light, as they all should be, and hits me straight in the heart. "I haven't even thought about my ankle since you made my body release all those endorphins."

With that testimonial, my cock roars fully to life and taps her leg. "Ignore that," I say, when her eyes open wide.

"What if I don't want to?" She grazes the tip with her fingers, pulling back when it jerks involuntarily from her touch. "Did I do it wrong? I don't want to hurt it. You."

"Your touch will never be wrong. Explore me however you want. Rhinos are very solidly built; you won't hurt me."

"I don't want to tease you, either," she says, pulling her bottom lip between her teeth. "I've always wanted you to be my first, but I'm not sure I'm brave enough yet to try."

Cupping her face, I sweep my thumb across her soft cheek. "You told me you believe things happen when it's time for them to happen. I believe in fate, too." *Tell her*, the voice of the mating bond demands again. It's time I listen. "I'll wait for you as long as you want me to. Whether that's five minutes, five years, or five decades. However long it takes, no matter what has to happen along the way. Because I don't care if I'm your first. I want to be your last."

"My last? As in—" Her lips close tight, as if she's fighting to keep more words from escaping.

"As in, I haven't just been physically attracted to you since the first time I saw you. It's more than that. Not all rhinos are fortunate enough to experience a true mate bond, but it's something we all hope for. I had no reason to leave my old home in the plains of Kenya, yet I was compelled to move halfway around the world to a mountaintop in Canada."

"You came here to buy a business from a retiring stoneworker. That's what you told Garion."

"The opportunity was a catalyst; I realized that the moment I saw you. The mating pull snapped into place, deep in my soul, and I knew you were the reason I came here. But I couldn't very well tell your gargoyle father that his nineteen-year-old human daughter was my fated mate."

"Because you thought I was too young, I know. But why, even after years passed, and I was older, did you always—" Shaking her head, she looks away, everywhere in the darkened room except at me.

"Why did I reject your attention at every turn?" I say, stroking her hair when she returns her attention to my face. "You deserve the freedom to live anywhere in the world with a husband who can walk by your side, no matter where you want to go. To have a houseful of beautiful babies who look like you. A full, human life. Now that I know your history, I understand why Garion has driven that point home every chance he gets. I think he's aware of my feelings and wanted to make sure I didn't pursue you because I can't give you the future you deserve."

The softness that's intrinsically Rose vanishes before my eyes. "How nice of you and Garion both to decide my future without once asking what I want. It's like I'm a powerless pawn in the game of my own life all over again." She brushes my hands away. "If I thought I could hop out of here without you intervening, I would, but since I know I'm not in control of that aspect of my life either, I'll sleep here tonight." Then she turns her back to me and moves to the edge of the bed, putting as much space between us as possible.

Even in the middle of winter, my bedroom has never felt so cold.

Six

ROSE

It's a relief and a disappointment to wake up in a silent house and find a note on the bedside table. Sunlight pours through the bedroom window, and when I reach for my phone to shut off my morning alarm, I know it's well past Cornelius's starting time for work. His days start a lot earlier than mine. After the late night we had, he's probably exhausted. I shouldn't care, I don't want to care, but I do.

I pretended not to notice when he left the bed after I rolled away from him last night. Then I tried to convince myself I didn't care about that, either. I've never been good at lying, especially to myself, and the tears that flowed out of me were an almost endless stream of proof. At least I managed to keep quiet. Bad enough that he's taken it upon himself to decide how I should feel and what I should want. Pity on top of that would be even worse.

Reaching for the note, my attention catches on the broom-handle walking stick I left out by the pool, now propped against the wall near the headboard. Either he's got mad tiptoe powers, or I was sleeping like the dead, because I didn't hear him moving around in here. Probably for the best. I'm still pissed off at him for all the assumptions he's made about me, but all the other feelings are still there, too. Even thinking about seeing him has tears building behind my eyes. Whatever happens next between us, I don't want it to include getting weepy in front of him. That'd just prove his point that I'm too young and sweet and blah, blah, blah.

"Ugh!" I roll onto my back, the folded paper clutched to my chest. I should leave the note unread and get on with my life. The life he thinks he shouldn't be part of, even though he claims I'm his fated mate. Contradiction much?

Sighing, I open the paper, a lump rising in my throat as I trail my fingers over my name written in tidy cursive.

Rose,

I'm not going to apologize on a piece of paper. I want to do that in person, if you let me, and when you're ready.

Since you can't drive until Dr. Schaefer says you can put weight on that foot, and I assumed you wouldn't want my help, I asked your friend Alexis to drive you to the doctor's office this morning. She'll be there at nine. If you're not at your store by its opening time, I'll go over and stick a note on the door telling customers you'll be back soon.

I spoke with the plumber, and he'll swing by your house after your shop closes today to look into your hot water issue. If he can't fix it on the spot, you're always welcome to use my facilities, and I will go run some errands while you do, so you have privacy.

There's a good chance you're going to be angry about all of those things because it probably seems like I'm making decisions for you again, trying to control your life. That's not my intention or motivation, but based on my previous behavior, I will understand if you see it that way.

If you need anything, anytime, let me know. I will always be here for you.

There's no sign-off, just a swooping line below the text.

It's not the groveling apology I was hoping for, but it's also not the breaking-things-off note I was afraid I might find. It's just Cornelius being Cornelius, doing what he thinks is best for me.

I know he didn't make those calls and plans out of some overbearing need to control my life. He did them because he cares for me. The same reason he kept his distance for the past five years, why he fought his feelings and kept them secret. Of course, *that* decision was wrong. But it was his to make.

Well…shit.

CORNELIUS

A busy day on the jobsite wasn't enough to keep my mind off of Rose. At the current stage of the stonework, I spent most of the day inside, without a sightline of Rose's flower shop.

Either lucky timing or fate had me near the renovation job's front window when she arrived, dropped off by her friend Alexis. It took everything in me not to rush over there. To help. To apologize. To make things right.

At five o'clock, I'm winding things down, cleaning up my area of the jobsite, when my phone pings with a new text. Could be anyone, and is most likely job-related, but my pulse kicks up with hope, like it has every time the phone buzzed in my pocket today. This time, when I swipe my thumb across the screen, the only name that matters is on my screen.

Rose
Your note said you want to talk. If you're free after work, can we talk then?

We can talk anytime you want. I'll walk away from anything for you.

Rose
I have things to do here at the shop, so no rush. Stop by when you're ready.

No rush. Stop by. Words people use for unimportant things. Casual meetups. The opposite of everything I feel and want.

Washing up. Be over in a few minutes.

Rose
I'll leave the front door unlocked for you. 🌹

No blushing face emoji this time. Just the rose. But it's something.

Ten minutes later, the old-fashioned bell over the door of Rose's Garden chimes my entrance. I've only been in one other time, for her grand opening three years ago, and there were so many bodies packed into the small space, all I could smell was people. With just Rose and I in the shop, I'm bombarded by scents of flowers and greenery. Fresh scents that remind me of Rose's hair, Rose's skin. I assumed it was her perfumes and products. Once again, I assumed wrong.

Standing at a worktable near the rear of the store, her long red hair shimmering beneath the over-hanging light, a pale-pink dress caressing her curves in a way that makes me envious of the fabric, she looks over her shoulder at me. "Would you turn the dead-bolt? I don't want anyone thinking I'm open and inter-rupting us."

Nodding, I lock the door, the metallic click of it sharp against the pounding pulse in my ears. "I saw you arrive on crutches. Any news from your appoint-ment with Dr. Schaefer?"

"The swelling has gone down a lot, but she did a

scan anyway, and confirmed it's just a minor sprain. I need to be careful with it, probably for a few weeks."

"That's good news. If there's anything I can do, I'm happy to."

"I know, thank you. And thank you for the arrangements you took the time to make. I'm not angry; I appreciate them."

"Glad I could help," is what I say. Internally, there's a celebration going on. Prematurely, maybe, but pebbles are something to build with, even though they're small.

"Your note said you wanted to talk face-to-face. I have something to say, too."

So much for hopeful pebbles. The words, *I have something to say*, are like a rock weighing heavy in my gut. Though, whatever she has to say, I have it coming.

"Ladies first."

"Not this time," she says, her mouth curving ever so slightly in a smile.

My mind immediately jumps to making her come last night, and my cock jumps right along with it. Uncouth thing doesn't give a shit about inappropriate timing. The thick, dark work pants don't offer much in the way of room to grow, but hopefully the compression will prevent her from noticing that I'm hard.

"You don't have to stand at the door." She waves me closer, then sets some eucalyptus sprigs and a pair of shears aside, turning to face me fully when I join her at the worktable.

"All night, all day today, I practiced what I'd say if you gave me the chance, and now that I have it, all the well-thought-out sentences are nowhere to be found."

"I don't care if it's fancy prose or bullet points or interpretive dance. Just be honest."

"If you'd ever seen a rhino dance, that wouldn't be an option. Not a pretty sight." The jab at myself earns me a light laugh and a small smile. "I'm sorry I hurt you. With rejection, lies of omission, and presumptuous jackassery. Holding myself back, and you at arm's length... I see now how it was controlling, but that was never my intention. I thought by removing myself as an option, I was doing what was best for you, what would make you happiest in your future. But the choice should always have been yours—I had no right to make it for you. I'm sorry I made assumptions and took the decision from you. I will always do whatever I can to take care of you, but *how* I take care of you is your choice now. Fate picked you as my mate, but my heart is yours because I love you."

For several slow, beautiful blue blinks, she's silent. Then she throws her arms around my neck, pressing her softness tight against me. "That was the most beautiful thing I've ever heard. Thank you."

Gods, she feels good in my arms. I can't believe I spent five years trying to prevent it. "I meant every word, Rose." I press a kiss to her soft hair, then thread my fingers through its silky length. "Maybe it's too soon for you to hear that I love you, but I don't want to keep what I feel inside anymore. You deserve to know everything."

"As much as I dreamed of hearing those words every day for the past five years, I really do believe things happen when it's the right time for them to happen."

"If I could go back—"

"We'd never get to have *this* moment," she says, smiling up at me, running her hands over my neck, my ears, my face, before placing her palms flat on my chest. "And I love this moment."

"Does that mean you forgive me? If you need more time or space, I'll wait. Not patiently, not easily, but respectfully."

"I don't want another minute of time or space without you right here," she says, sliding her arms around me again. "And I had already forgiven you, before your beautiful speech. My past reared its big ugly head last night. It really hurt to find out you'd deprived me of the freedom to choose who I spend my life with. The hurt ballooned and pushed everything else aside. This morning, when I read your note, I realized I owe you an apology, too. I wasn't angry solely because you took my choice away. I was also angry because you didn't do what *I* thought was best. If I could have controlled things to get what I wanted, I would have. Just because I didn't actually do it doesn't make me less guilty. I'm sorry for blowing up at you."

"You had every right to."

"Maybe, but I still wish I hadn't. Apparently, escaping my mafia father didn't mean outrunning my hotheaded Sicilian roots."

"That fiery spirit is why you're in my arms. I needed it. I love it and every other part of you."

"And I love you. Every part of you. Including the part I was a bit afraid of last night, but I'm not anymore." Bright pink floods her beautiful, fair face. "I talked to Dr. Schaefer about it today. She assured me we'll fit together, and said just to make sure I'm well lubricated and that I've been, um, prepped, to make accommodating your size pleasurable."

"*Rose.*" It comes out raw and gravelly. Pretty sure my cock is harder than any other time in my entire life. As much as I want to show her exactly how pleasurable I'll make it when I'm deep inside her, it's her other words that matter most—she loves me. Gently, I cup her face in my hand, tipping her chin up and angling my head to kiss her. Carefully. Deeply.

Like the first time, her taste hits me hard, igniting the mating bond. Only now that neither of us is holding anything back, it's fully open. The heat between us is more than physical chemistry, more than the innate need to breed with her. It's everything. She's everything.

Breaking the kiss, she pulls back enough that our eyes meet. "Last night, you said part of why you denied what you felt is because you wanted me to have a houseful of human babies. Maybe it's because I was an only child, motherless, and basically fatherless too, since he had little to do with me, but having kids has never been more than a fuzzy possibility. *Gray* and fuzzy, I realized this morning. So, I asked Dr. Schaefer about that, too. She said our DNA is compatible, and the female human body is capable of carrying and delivering a human-rhino baby, if that's something we want one day."

Just when I thought my heart couldn't get fuller, Rose makes it feel as if it could burst from my chest. "You asked the doctor about having children with me."

"I thought we should have all the information, just in case. If you never want kids, I'll get on birth control before we take the next step."

"This is one choice that only you should make, and no matter what you decide, I'll still be the happiest man to walk the earth because I'm walking with you."

"Then...you're okay with leaving it up to nature to decide? Dr. Schaefer said that despite biological compatibility, cross-species reproduction isn't a sure thing. I could get pregnant the first time, or it might never happen, no matter how much we want it to or try."

Straining against the inside of my pants, my cock proves that it can indeed get harder.

"We can talk later; we should probably get going since you arranged for the plumber." The glassiness in her eyes and flush of pink high on her cheeks tell a different story than her well-intentioned words.

"The plumber can wait. I can't."

A soft gasp leaves her parted lips as I grip her waist and lift her onto the worktable. "Here?" she says when I gather her dress in my hands and pull it up to pool at her hips.

"I'm not going to fuck you here. Not today, anyway. But I need to taste you and feel you come. Right now."

"What if someone looks through the front window?"

"They'll see us hugging and kissing, be happy for us, and move along."

"If your face is between my legs, only one of us will be kissing."

I chuckle at the adorable eyebrow wiggle she gives me. "There's more than one way to taste you." I press two fingers against the thin strip of material covering her pussy, running my knuckles up and down until she's rocking against my touch and I feel her wetness through the fabric. Then I tug the panties from her body and bring them to my face, groaning as I inhale her intimate scent.

Her eyes open wider when I drag my tongue over the material. Then she gasps as I take the section that's damp with her juices into my mouth and suck it, a rumble vibrating from deep inside me.

"Delicious," I say, tucking the panties into my

pocket while stepping between her knees. "My sweet Rose." Rolling the pad of my thumb back and forth over her clit, I cup her face with the other hand and press my mouth to her soft lips.

She parts for me, a throaty *mmm* vibrating against my tongue when I slide it alongside hers. Back arched, she tips her hips up, her body rocking in time with my rhythm on her clit. She breaks the kiss, whispering, "Harder," through choppy breaths.

I give her what she needs while sliding one finger inside her, then adding a second, her pussy hugging my fingers like a vise.

"More," she pants, moaning when I ease three fingers into her tight wet heat while working my thumb faster and harder over her clit. Her mouth falls open, her beautiful, erotic cries of pleasure filling the air.

"Gods, you're beautiful," I say when the last ripple runs through her and she snuggles against my chest. "I was such a fool to think I could have a life without you."

"Good thing I smartened you up." Chin digging into my chest, she tilts her head to meet my gaze. "Take me to my house? Now that I'm not selfishly and thoroughly indulging in your touch, I feel bad keeping your plumber friend waiting."

"I'll make it up to him with beers at The Brew. How about I tell him to stop by another day, and you and I can go share a nice, long wallow in the big tub before I take you to bed and make you come until I've wrung every last orgasm out of your beautiful, sexy body."

A fresh wave of rosy pink blooms on her face, her smile stretching nearly ear to ear. "If you do that, I might never want to go home."

Or maybe she'll decide that she's already there.

Seven

ROSE

It's happening. Tonight.

I know Cornelius will be okay if I change my mind and tell him I'm not ready. But I am ready. I've been ready to have this night with him since the first time I met him. Except, on that day, I had no idea how huge his cock was. And I should have at least *guessed* it'd be huge, because by that point, I'd been in Lexi's store, and Every Witch Way sells some obscenely large dildos, all of which are molded from real penises. But she didn't have a rhino man model, so my naïve nineteen-year-old brain just pictured Cornelius having a standard human cock, except in gray.

Oh, how wrong I was.

The water shuts off in the bathroom, and my pulse goes into overdrive, filling my ears with a staccato beat. The Jack and Jill door opens and Cornelius steps into the bedroom with a towel around his waist, the fluffy white terry barely reining in his erection. It's like he has a tent pole under there. Only the pole is made from one of those trees with the freakishly large girth.

"You look pale. And shaky." Cornelius doesn't have eyebrows, but the movement of his ears is a telltale sign of concern. "When did you last eat? How about I carry you to the kitchen and make you dinner?"

"I don't think I could eat right now," I say, fiddling with the tie of my itty-bitty robe.

"Then I'll carry you to the tub, help you get settled, and leave you to relax in private—but please call for me when you're ready to get out."

"And then what?"

"Then whatever you want to happen happens. Dinner. Television. Talking. Crafts. Cuddling. Or I can sleep in the guest room and give you space."

"I don't want space—did you say crafts?" I ask, giggling when he nods. "What would you do if I choose crafts?"

"Get my supplies out of the closet."

He has to be teasing.

"What kind of supplies?"

"Crochet and modeling clay." His mouth curves up at the corners when my bottom lip drops. "I'm not great at either, but better at crocheting. I mostly make balls with the clay." Chuckling, he shrugs. "Rolling clay between my palms is very relaxing."

"And the crocheting? Do you have one incredibly long chain stitch going?"

"I've progressed from the single chain." A twinkle lights his gray eyes. "I made the blanket I threw over you when you flashed me on the couch."

An indignant huff bursts from my lips. "*That* was an accident. Out at the pool, *that* was flashing." Memories from last night play in my mind, melting away the nervousness from a few minutes ago. I know tonight will be amazing because he'll make it that way. "It's a beautiful blanket. I never would've guessed you made it."

"There's a lot we don't know about each other yet," he says, leaning against the doorframe. "And we have many decades to learn it all. There's no rush, Rose."

I know he's not referring to our hobbies and interests. Not really. He's letting me know it's okay if we take our time in the bedroom. Or bathroom, since that was first on tonight's list.

"I'd like to learn how to crochet if you're willing to teach me, but not tonight. Tonight, I want you to teach me other things I've never done."

"Anything you want."

"I want you to drop the towel." The words have barely left my mouth when the towel falls to the floor, leaving him fully naked in front of me. "Come closer."

As big and heavy as he is, his footfalls are practically silent on the hardwood floor as he closes the distance between us, leaving enough space for me to see everything in clear detail.

"I don't know where to look first," I say, and he chuckles again. My face heats like I'm too close to the fire. Which makes sense, because Cornelius is the hottest man I have ever seen.

Gray all over—except for his cock—even the smoothest areas of his skin are textured, while other areas have a more pronounced bumpiness, and the skin on his shoulders and chest has a heavy, almost structured look. Heavily muscled, even in his thick middle, he exudes power.

I know he's incredibly strong; I've seen him lift ridiculously large rocks with his bare hands. Even without all his muscles, he's huge. The thought of him on top of me, pressing all that bulk against me while he fucks me, sends sparks racing between my legs.

Watching me with patient eyes, he waits for my gaze to drop below his thick middle, then opens his stance. His cock bobs with the shift in position, the hard length of it slapping against his midsection.

The tip isn't a smooth taper, it's almost blunt, with a ringlike shape at the top that has rounded bumps, sort of like a smoothed-out crown. Below that is a heavily veined section about the width of my hand. Then there are...I don't know what exactly. Fins? Wings?

An audible gulp escapes before I can swallow it down.

He reaches for me, his big hand slipping under my chin, tipping it up so I'm looking into his kind eyes, not at his one-eyed monster. "Spending my life with you is all I need to be happy."

I curl my fingers around his shaft. "I want to raise the bar for 'happy.'"

He groans as I trace the smooth, bumpy ring with the pad of my thumb, then slide my hand down, exploring the textured, protruding ridges on either side. "Consider it raised." His enjoyment of my simple touch is exactly what I need to feel like a siren instead of a nervous little virgin.

"Tell me if I do something that doesn't feel good," I say, backing up carefully and settling on the small bench at the end of the bed.

"Anything you want to do is going to feel amazing to me." He draws a deep breath when I take his cock in both hands, moving them up and down the thick, silky, lower portion before gripping the two protruding ridges like handles. "Really fucking amazing." He groans again when I guide him to my mouth and trail my tongue over the crowned tip, then scoop the milky bead of precum at the center.

Another bead quickly takes its place, and I lap that one up too, *mmming* at the fresh, sweet taste of him on my tongue. Looking up his body, our gazes lock, and I open wide, encircling the head of his cock with my lips.

His breath rushes out in a husky rasp as I guide him deeper into my mouth. The ridges I'm holding bump against the corners of my mouth, preventing me from taking any more of him. *"Gods, Rose,"* he rasps when I swallow the ambrosial precum dribbling down my throat. Then he threads one hand through my hair and gently eases me off his cock. "What you're doing feels amazing, but I don't want to come in your mouth the first time you give me the privilege of being inside it."

Butterflies flap wildly in my belly as he scoops me into his arms. Placing my palms on his chest, I feel his heart racing, too. "I want you," I say softly, sliding my hands over every inch of skin I can reach. It's like leather and concrete combined, and as he carries me to the bathroom, the subtle abrasion of it against my nipples tightens the longing building inside me. "I want to be with you, to feel you inside me."

"Whatever you want, Rose, it's yours." After gently setting me on my feet, he tugs the bow at my waist and slides the silky robe off my shoulders, letting it flutter to the floor. "You're so beautiful," he says, lifting me again, then setting me in the tub. "How's the temperature?"

"Perfect." I curl my legs to my chest to make room when he doesn't join me. "Is the water too hot?" It's to my liking, but he told me rhinos prefer it cool.

"I'd get into boiling lava for you." The water level rises from half to full when he settles his huge, mouth-watering body across from me, his arms along the curved backrest and his legs fully extended, one foot gently stroking my hip. In this position, the wavy motion of the water makes his cock look like a submerged marble statue.

When I look up, he's watching me. Calmly. Patiently. But also, hungrily. He crooks a finger at me. "Come here, beautiful."

Moving toward him, I almost can't hear the gentle ripple of water over the pound of my heartbeat. "I don't know what to do," I whisper when his hands find my waist and pull me flush against him.

"Whatever feels good." Gliding one hand up my back, he cups my head and guides my mouth to his. His tongue slips between my lips and his horn presses against the side of my face, reminding me of the pleasure he gave me when he had me grinding my clit on it.

I follow the rhythm of the kiss, pressing my pussy against his rock-hard length. The thick width of it spreads me, my clit roaring to life at the contact.

His chest rumbles, the vibrations radiating through me. The hand at my waist travels down to my backside, kneading my squishy flesh before sliding between my legs.

I gasp into his mouth when his finger slides inside my pussy, then whimper when it withdraws.

"I'm going to give you everything you need," he says, entering me with two fingers, then, on the next stroke, adding another. He swivels his wrist, making his fingertips brush against something inside me that has me rocking against him. "One more, beautiful." Before it registers in my brain, his fingers withdraw, then slide inside me again, stretching me wider.

One more.

Four long, thick fingers fill me, the base of them nestled between my lips. I'm so full, but I want more. I need more. Gripping his shoulders, I grind on him, rolling my clit along his shaft. With each downward movement, his hand eases deeper inside me, filling me with an erotic burn. The first flicker of orgasm tingles beneath my clit, then goes off like a bomb inside me. Panting and writhing, I come until I can barely breathe from the onslaught of pleasure.

His fingers slip out of me as the last ripple of orgasm fades, then his hands are on my waist again, lifting me, guiding my entrance to the head of his cock. He doesn't push inside or pull me onto him, just looks into my eyes and waits, giving me the choice.

"Yes." The word leaves me on a breath as I wiggle downward. The tip of his cock slips inside me easily. Then those two protruding ridges press against my labia, stretching me open to take them. "Oh, gods..." I moan as their hard, bumpy texture ignites every nerve ending they touch. And when they press against that extra-sensitive spot inside me, I cry out as I come, hard and fast.

"I love it when you come." His deep, gravelly voice sends a shiver through me. Holding me tight, he pushes deeper inside me, then eases back and goes even deeper. In and out, in and out, each stroke dragging his ridges over sensitive spots I didn't know I had, pushing me closer to coming again. "You feel good, squeezing me so tight, taking me so deep."

"More," I pant, even though I don't know how I can possibly take more of him inside me. But I want it. I need it. "Please."

One big thumb finds my clit, rubbing it fast and hard, pushing me into another orgasm as he thrusts impossibly deeper. Grinding and jerking against him, I pant and moan, riding the endless wave of climax. Water slaps against us, our fucking sending it sloshing out of the tub.

"Fuck," he groans, the hand on my hip gripping me tight, holding me in place as heat flares inside me, his cock throbbing and expanding until I gasp from the fullness of it.

"What-what's happening?"

"The bloom," he says, wrapping his arms around my back and holding me against his chest, his hips still pumping his cock inside me. "It won't last long, but I can't stop it. Does it hurt?"

"No, it's—" My breath stutters as the spiral hits, and I'm coming *again*, this one a slow wave of sensual bliss that doesn't end until his cock stops fluttering inside me. "What was that?"

"The bloom," he says again, kissing my forehead. "That ring at the head of my cock flares when I come."

"Oh! Like a flower blooming."

"Exactly like that."

"That's kind of perfect, isn't it, with me being your Rose?"

He gently lifts my chin, a smile on his face when our eyes meet. "It is, and you are."

"The bloom, does it happen every time?" I ask, trailing my fingers over his wet, leathery skin. Just thinking about it brings my clit online, and I wiggle on top of him to get some pressure.

"Every time, my sweet Rose." Still buried inside me, his cock thickens. Then his hands are on my hips, and he's stroking deep inside me again, sending water slapping onto the bathroom floor.

A week or so later

CORNELIUS

I'm already out of bed and pulling on pants by the time Rose lifts her sleepy head from the pillow at the heavy rap of knuckles on the front door. The sound of heavy feet landing on the driveway next door woke me faster than any weekday alarm ever has.

"Is someone knocking?" She reaches for her phone from the side table, making an adorable huff when she sees the time. "Who in the world is at our door at six on a Sunday morning?"

Our door. If I had time, I would show her how much her use of "our" means to me.

"Your father."

Her eyes look as if they might pop out of her head. "Shit! What is he doing here? He's not supposed to be back for another week!" She tosses the covers off and lunges from the bed.

Before her feet touch the ground, I have my arms around her waist, catching her to prevent the impact. Her ankle is getting stronger by the day, but it's a long way from being one hundred percent. The last thing we need right now is for her to reinjure it while naked, with her father, who isn't aware of the change to his daughter's relationship status, waiting at the front door.

"Thank you," she says, pulling me down by the horn and caressing it while kissing me.

"Don't wake the monster." I peel her soft fingers from my horn. "I doubt your father would appreciate me greeting him with a hard-on."

"Too late." She giggles while checking out the bulge behind my fly. "Sorry?"

"You don't look the least bit sorry," I say with a chuckle, then give her a quick kiss before stepping away from temptation.

Another sharp knock on the front door startles the smile off of her face. "What should we do?"

Something inside me deflates. This isn't how I envisioned revealing our relationship to Garion, but I did assume we'd tell him as soon as he returned from Sicily. "The choice is yours. What do you want to do?"

"The choice is *ours*, isn't it?" She wraps her arms around her middle, a defensive posture I haven't seen her take since I pulled my head out of my ass and told her how I feel about her. "Unless you're not sure what you want."

With one step, I'm in front of her, tugging her against me and stroking her long, silky hair while kissing her head. "You're the center of every waking thought and every nightly dream. The past week has been the happiest of my life, and I want it to be the first week of forever with you. There is nothing I'm more sure about."

She tips her head back, eyes shining, full lips curved in a smile more beautiful than any flower could ever be. "Then I should get dressed so we can answer the door together."

The next round of insistent knocking rattles the wood as I'm setting Rose on her feet at the front door.

She doesn't take a big breath or hesitate in any way; she just grabs the handle and flings the door open wide. "You're back!" Genuine joy lights her face at the sight of her adoptive father.

"*Dusci mia,*" Garion says, stepping forward to hug her. Looking over her shoulder at me, his yellow eyes meet mine, but give nothing away. Releasing her, his gaze falls from her face. "What happened? I left you intact."

Rose swallows, a loud gurgling sound audible in her throat, and her cheeks flare with a red blush.

"She sprained her ankle," I say, when Rose remains tongue-tied. "Dr. Schaefer did a scan the next day and says it's minor, but Rose has been careful to keep her weight off of it, including letting me drive her to and from the flower shop."

"Thank you for seeing she was well taken care of." Garion turns his attention to Rose. "Why didn't you mention this in your messages?"

"Because you would've asked how it happened,

and I didn't want to lie to you, or tell you the truth, while you were halfway around the world." With a careful hop, she's by my side, her arms wrapped around my middle. "I slipped while getting out of Cornelius's tub. Well, it was Cornelius's tub when I slipped," she says, then looks up at me, a wide, loving smile curving her beautiful pink lips. "Now it's our tub."

Garion's brow line rises. At his back, his wings twitch, and I hold my breath, waiting for them to unfurl and the claws to come out, literally. Garion has never shown any sign of temper in the five years I've known him, but gargoyles are ferocious when in protector mode.

If I had a beautiful, innocent daughter and came home from a trip to find she'd been deflowered by the monster I'd asked to look out for her, I'd probably ram my horn through his chest. Or lower, where he really deserved to feel the pain.

"I love your daughter," I say, breaking the silence hanging between us. "I've known she's my true mate since the day I met her, and I spent five long years fighting my instincts and feelings. I thought about moving, leaving Fate's Falls, but even if I couldn't be with her as her mate, I couldn't be away from her, either. I truly tried to respect your wishes of a full, human life for Rose. Every time I rejected her, it killed a piece of my soul. I hated hurting her, and I'll never do it again. All I want to do is love, provide, and cherish her for the rest of my life, and she has honored me by saying yes."

"And you, Rose?" Garion asks.

"He's the only one I've ever wanted. The only person who's ever made my heart race and my soul feel alive. I love Cornelius and, if fate hadn't brought us together, I'm sure, without a doubt, there would never be anyone else for me."

Garion's gray lips shift, rising at one corner. "Fate brought you both to Fate's Falls. Fate even went so far as to drop you next door to each other. But I get the credit for bringing you together."

"*You?* But you told Cornelius I deserve a full, human life."

"I did say those words, yes. Because I wanted Cornelius to give you that life. The full, human experience of opening yourself to someone, trusting them, loving them with your whole heart and being loved the same way. The experience of having a family, if you choose to. Gargoyles are no strangers to the mate bond. I sensed on the day he arrived that Cornelius was meant to be that person for you."

"All those times you told me what you wanted for Rose," I say, meeting Garion's yellow eyes, "I focused on the word 'human,' not 'full.' I thought you were subtly warning me away because you wanted her to be with a human." Five years lost to assumptions. Five years I could have spent with Rose.

"Things happen when they're supposed to happen," she says, as if reading my mind.

Garion grunts a laugh. "Or when your father gives things a nudge by going out of town after removing an integral, yet difficult to diagnose, part from the hot water heater, and ensuring your adoring, devoted neighbor would come to the rescue."

Rose's bottom lip drops. "You broke the water heater on purpose?"

"It's not broken. Just temporarily sabotaged. The headwinds last night were terrible, so I'm going home to fix the water heater so I can have a hot shower before sleeping for eight hours." He leans in, kisses Rose's cheek, then offers his hand for me to shake. "Welcome to the family."

"It's a pleasure and an honor to be part of it," I say, Rose squeezing my middle as I clasp Garion's hand.

"Dad, wait," she calls as he's walking away.

The smile on his face when he turns is pure love. Garion didn't just rescue her eleven years ago, he gave her the experience she should have had for the first thirteen years of her life—to be loved unconditionally by a parent. To have that parent do whatever is necessary for their child to have a full, happy life.

And she loves him right back.

She hops to the doorway and leans out, the ends of her long red locks dancing in the morning breeze. "How do you know I haven't had the water heater fixed already?"

"I paid the plumber not to fix it until I got home," he says. "Like I said before, I'm taking credit for this one." With a nod and a wave, he crosses the yards and enters the house next door. His house now, not theirs.

"Welcome home," I say against Rose's ear, pulling her tight to me after locking *our* front door. "Join me for a morning wallow, then breakfast in bed?"

"I'd love that." Smiling at me, she wraps her arms around the back of my neck when I scoop her off her feet. "What's for breakfast?"

"You, my sweet Rose. And I'm starving, so prepare to be devoured."

Thank you for reading Cornelius and Rose's fated mates love story! I hope you enjoyed this sweet and spicy nugget of fluffy, feel-good romance.

There are lots of happily ever afters happening in the secret monster town of Fate's Falls! Go back and visit the town's residents soon in these stories:

Mated to the Minotaur
The Grumpy Demon's Sunshine
A Reaper is Forever
and more steamy, cozy stories coming soon!

Join Karla Doyle's mailing list and stay up to date on new releases, bonus content, sales, freebies, contests, and more.
www.karladoyle.com/newsletter

Contemporary Romances:

Wedded Miss

Dad Bod Wingman (Hope Harbor)

Heart Beats (Hope Harbor)

Last Call Casanova (Hope Harbor)

Fleshing It Out (Hope Harbor)

The Deal With Love (Hope Harbor)

Doggy Style (Hope Harbor)

Resorting to Love (linked to Hope Harbor)

White Lie Christmas (linked to Hope Harbor)

King of Her Dreams (Hope Harbor)

Heart of Texas (linked to Hope Harbor)

Her Pipe Dream (Hope Harbor)

12 Days (Hope Harbor)

Puck That

Shifting Gears (Under the Hood)

Driver's Seat (Under the Hood)

Gingerbread Man (Man of the Month: Candy Cane Key)

Just in Queso (Man of the Month: Magnolia Point)

Unexpected Addition

Dating the Doubter

Gift Wrapped

Cup of Sugar (Close to Home #1)

Icing on the Cake (Close to Home #2)

Sweet as Candy (Close to Home #3)

Body of Work (Very Personal Training #1)

Worth the Wait (Very Personal Training #2)

Game Plan

More Than Words

Crossing the Line

Visit Karla's website for the most up-to-date list.

www.karladoyle.com

Click here to see Karla's books sorted by tropes and themes!

www.karladoyle.com/books/by-tropes/

About the Author

A small-town girl with some big-city experience, Karla resides in Southwestern Ontario with her husband and two amazing, young-adult kids. She studied fashion design in college and spent 20+ years working in that industry before succumbing to the writing muse. When she's not writing the sexy stories that swirl around in her head, you can find her spending time with family, hanging out with book-loving friends on Facebook, or cuddled up with a book and her adorable pets.

Karla loves hearing from readers! Connect with her online, or send her an email: karla@karladoyle.com.

Join Karla's mailing list to stay up
to date on all her news.
www.karladoyle.com/newsletter/

facebook.com/KarlaDoyleAuthor

instagram.com/KarlaDoyleAuthor

tiktok.com/@karladoyleauthor

bookbub.com/authors/karla-doyle

goodreads.com/karlad

youtube.com/@KarlaDoyleAuthor

bsky.app/profile/karladoyleauthor.bsky.social

patreon.com/KarlaDoyleAuthor

Want more cozy monster romances?

Go on an adventure to the secret town of Fate's Falls and fall in love with all of its irresistible monster mates! All books take place in Fate's Falls, and you'll see some character appearances and familiar town landmarks. Each book is a standalone romance with a different couple and their journey to a very happily ever after.

Mated to the Minotaur
The Grumpy Demon's Sunshine
A Reaper is Forever
The Rhino's Rose
A Dash of Demon
Hell's Belle
Orc-ily Ever After
Falling for the Yeti

...and more to come!

This book was written by a human.
Every sentence came
directly from the mind of the author.

**This author does not use or support
AI-generated content.**